THE LIBRARY OF SOULS

THE LIBRARY

OF SOULS

RICHARD DENNEY

THE LIBRARY OF SOULS

Summary: When thirteen-year-old Simon Santiago, who can talk to the dead, arrives at one of the most haunted libraries in the world to get rid of its malicious spirits, he quickly finds out that things are not what they seem.

[Juvenile fiction – Paranormal – Horror – Friendship – Family – Ghosts – Adventure – Mystery and detective stories]

ISBN: 978-1539149880

Printed and bound in the U.S.A.

For my devoted readers &
Booktube viewers!

PROLOGUE:
WHAT YOU NEED TO KNOW FIRST.

I can talk to dead people... no, you didn't read wrong. It's 100% true.

When my parents died when I was nine, I was sent to live with my estranged uncle in New York City. You might think, *at least you're not an orphan,* but see I'd never met my uncle Monty before and my dad didn't really have a stable enough relationship with him to leave me with my uncle. They practically hated each other. But how would my parents know that their train was going to crash into another and end their lives as well as hundreds of others? They hadn't even created a will yet.

A few days later I was on a plane to New York and had to take a taxi on my own to a shabby looking brownstone that looked as if it were about to collapse at any moment. I had to carry my own luggage up those cracked concrete steps and ring the button that read: *Santiago* in sloppy red marker.

I kind of regret ever pushing that button. I wish I would've known the insanity that would become my life. I wish I knew that I would never go back to school or make any friends or have any type of life of my own, because once I stepped foot into Uncle Monty's dank apartment that smelt of rotting Chinese food and dirty socks, I belonged to him.

My uncle Monty was a con-artist and a real good one at that. True, he wore his tie backwards and couldn't comb down that godforsaken cowlick on the right side of his head to save his life, but he was good at conning people out of whatever he desired. But he also liked to gamble his money away and spend a majority of it on trying to figure out why he couldn't talk to the dead. He was born normal out of a family of Mediums or Ghost Talkers, as I like to call myself and couldn't live with it. So he changed himself and made everyone hate him instead.

He was good once, I remember my dad telling my mom before they died. But it's hard to believe that when he makes me sleep on a busted twin mattress with no box spring in a room with foul smelling supernatural objects.

I, myself am a Ghost Talker. It took me until I was eight to be able to control my ability, which is young for people like me. But once in a while a spirit will just pop up

7

and scare the living daylights out of me, which is how my uncle found out I had the ability.

A week after I had come to live with him, I was cleaning out a giant luggage trunk full supernatural objects. Some with the price tags still on them from one of the many spiritualist shops my uncle had visited. I had been pulling out a jar of what looked like blue mucus, when a terrifying face slammed itself up against the glass and screamed at me.

I dropped it and it shattered on the ground expelling a truly revolting smell out of it, along with a disembodied ghost. I was running around my uncle's office for what felt like forever trying to catch the ghost in an empty mayonnaise jar. But it was no use. That thing was relentless. It wasn't until I heard a congratulatory slow clap that I knew I had been watched the whole time.

Uncle Monty stood in the doorway of his office and continued to slow clap.

"I knew you had the gift," he said as a large, menacing grin began to spread across his face. It was then I knew my life would never be the same. Of course talking to the dead didn't really count as being somewhat normal, but it was as close to it as I could get and in that instant, it had all come crashing down upon me like a pile of ghostly bricks.

From then on, I was his puppet of sorts. He created his own ghost busting agency that he had the audacity to call *Monty Santiago: Spirit expeller.* He pulled me out of school with the false intentions to home school me and we traveled all around the United States, me kindly asking ghosts to keep it down, while Uncle Monty pocketed the payments he got for his services. I was lucky if he threw me a twenty dollar bill from time to time.

In next to no time we were one of the top agencies in the U.S. and Monty even got his picture in the papers and in online magazines. But no one knew it was really me that did all the hard work. Why didn't I rat him out? Because of two reasons: he'd send me to a wayward home ran by someone he personally knew where I'd be treated way worse... and as much as it pained me, he was family.

No matter how much he told me that I didn't deserve the gift, or threatened me to get rid of a ghost or two, I did understand that with him, I was better off. I still however couldn't help but be angry with my parents and no matter how much I tried, I could never get a hold of them. I just wanted to ask them why they left me, and why they left me with *him.*

Soon years had passed and I turned thirteen. I

couldn't really solve a math problem to save my life or tell you what a neutron was (I still don't really know), but I could read twelve books in a week. I grew to love books. They helped me get through my uncle's rage-filled rants and the loneliness from not being able to make friends because we moved around so much. I loved books more than anything, so when one rainy October morning we got a call from a librarian in Massachusetts about one of the most haunted libraries in the world, I jumped at the chance, even if I still had no choice but to go.

Who was to know that it would be one of the most traumatic, horrifying, life-changing, and thrilling adventures of a lifetime?

-From the journal of Simon Santiago.

CHAPTER 1:
THE GIRL IN THE WINDOW

The library was massive as heck. I had to take several steps back, almost tripping over the curb into the street to take it all in. I had done the basic research online, going through dozens of videos of people filming their experiences in the building and several older articles from the 50s about children going in and never coming out. The Childermass Public Library had been built in 1886 by Jonathon R. Childermass, even the town was named after him. Of course it had been built over one of the largest and most overcrowded cemeteries in the United States. That's the best ingredient to a perfect ghost story.

Jonathon had the bodies exhumed and moved to a few neighboring cemeteries but since it was so overcrowded, plenty of bodies were left behind, some merely bones and ash. Even after being told numerous times that building over a cemetery was a curse in itself and three of his daughters dying mysteriously, the man did not let his dream of a massive library go.

Soon after the library had its grand opening, the rest of his children died under another set of mysterious circumstances during the same month. It wasn't until his wife had gone ill and quickly died that he began to believe the curse. Gossip spread quicker than wildfire and the library stayed empty. No one had showed up for months. Months later he'd finally driven himself mad and to save the rest of his family from the curse's grasps, he invited every single member of his family to his library and poisoned all of them.

Afterward he hung himself from the main chandelier in the circulation area of the library. The building had been closed down until 1952 when a sparred distant relative inherited the library and reopened it to the public once again. Ever since its reopening in 1952, many children have gone into the building never to be seen again. People have died from falling over the balcony of the second floor, and rumor has it a well known serial killer used its basement to carry out his crazed obscenities. And let's not forget to mention the never-ending hauntings. There were so many articles and videos on this, it would take me weeks to get through it all.

You'd think after all of this, they'd finally close it down and demolish the building, but as it turns out, the city loves the attention. There's even a gift shop on the main shopping street where you can buy a ghost in a jar, though the ghosts in the jars obviously aren't real, the city still makes loads of money off of tourists and television networks wanting to film at the library, which is why no one knew we were coming here. The librarian on the phone specifically asked that this be kept under wraps, because if the city found out they were trying to get rid of their ever-lasting money source, it would not end well for anyone.

So Monty had the librarian up the amount that he'd be paid for his visit and she was all too glad to do it. I had to admit that this would've been perfect publicity for Monty's agency, but he cared more about the money than anything else. It was his thing.

The library looked like a manor and a church had a baby. It was made out of dark gray stone and looked dilapidated and in fact, haunted. There were two gigantic stained glass windows on both sides of the double-door front entrance, and several smaller stained glass windows above the entrance's eave. Gargoyles and faces were carved into the stone, some looking almost life-like. There was definitely some supernatural vibes going on with the library.

It was also one of the most fascinating buildings I'd ever seen. At the roof of the building, it was fenced with black speared bars and below sat three wide windows that seemed to be glowing. It took me a few seconds to realize that there were candelabras in each of the windows.

The steps leading up to the doorway were made of stone as well and were cracked and gaping in parts, as if the building had been through an insane earthquake just recently. This place was most definitely old.

I pulled out my digital camera from my shoulder bag and began snapping photos of the building, hoping I'd get something on camera. Not only was I a massive reader, I also happened to love collecting spooky vintage photos and taking some of my own to keep in albums. It was a hobby of sorts.

I was taking a photo of one of the large stained glass windows opposite the double-door entrance, when Uncle Monty smacked the camera out of my hand. Luckily I already had the strap fitted around my neck.

"Put that thing away!" Monty growled at me, his caterpillar-like eyebrows bunched together in irritation. "We need to look professional."

"You know I like my photos," I said lifting the camera up to my face once again. "And that pink tie you're wearing doesn't really make us seem professional."

I peered up at my uncle and saw that he was fuming, but since we were in a public place, he'd keep it strictly PG and not yell at me or swat me in the back of the head. He pulled out his phone and quickly dialed the librarian. He had a thing for liking to be escorted into the haunt. He thought it made him seem more professional and real, when really all it made him look like was a jerk.

Peering back through my camera's lens, I fixed the focus back on one of the stained glass windows. As the blurriness cleared, a nearly transparent girl stood in the middle of the window. She was shaking her head and pointing to where Monty's Buick sat in the library's parking lot. Why was she telling us to leave? Even if I begged Monty to ditch this job, he wouldn't budge, he'd more than likely force me to go inside, and then scold me back at the hotel. I'd never hear the end of it.

Before the girl could vanish, I snapped a quick shot of her and looked at the display screen, hoping I'd caught something. And I did. It was one of the most perfect photos I'd ever taken. Quickly I swung the strap off my neck and held the camera up to Monty.

"I got a good one. She's telling us to leave too."

15

Monty snatched the camera from my hand and rolled his eyes before settling them on the display screen. The irritated look he had vanished and was replaced with pure awe.

This was the only way he'd be able to see the dead. I could tell it pained him that he wasn't like me and I almost felt sorry for him. But then I remembered how he treated me.

"That is a good one," he grinned. "We'll put it on the site. And we're not going anywhere. This is good money, kid. Good, good money!"

As if on cue, both of the gigantic front entrance doors to the library swung inward, groaning like distressed spirits. A frosty breeze fluttered down the steps and coiled itself around my ankles, seemingly pulling me toward the dark abyss that was the doorway.

For the first time in a long time, a bundle of chills spun down my spine like spiders made of ice. This was bad, *really* bad.

A woman, slim and tall walked out from the darkness of the interior and looked as if she were floating down the stone steps. She looked like a librarian with her pitch black hair up in a tight bun, a chunky pair of brown glasses resting on her bird-like nose, and she was wrapped in a cardigan that was the color of puke. She had a kind face and was giving off a warmth, that of a good person. I could sense it. She must've been Octavia Freestone, the librarian who'd called us.

She looked down at me first and smiled.

"You didn't tell me that your assistant was a child," the woman said, still not looking at Monty. I wasn't a child. Technically I was a teenager. There's a difference.

"I'm thirteen," I said, a bit annoyed. Yeah, I was short for my age but I still wasn't a kid. I couldn't even count the many times I'd been mistaken for a nine-year-old. At least it got me free dessert at restaurants from time to time.

"I'm sorry, young man. You look so young. It's not a bad thing though, it just means you'll still look young when you're my age." She sniggered and finally looked up at my uncle. I could see her blush and I wanted to stick my tongue out and shove a finger down my throat.

"Good afternoon, Montgomery Santiago." Ms. Freestone gleamed. Monty's real name is Montoya, but he changed it so it would sound more white. He said it's better for business. I just think it's stupid. Sometimes I wish my ability gave me the power to get rid of ignorant people than ghosts. This world would be so much better off.

My uncle straightened himself up real quick and showcased his brand new white teeth he'd bought with the money from our last job.

"Call me Monty," he smiled back.

"Like Monty Python?" Ms. Freestone tilted her head and giggled. I was truly getting grossed out watching them flirt. I wanted to get inside. I wanted to see all of the books. I wanted to talk to that ghost girl from the window.

"I love that movie." My uncle was terrible at flirting and it was almost too painful to watch. More than likely sensing my disdain for their flirt war Ms. Freestone looked down at me and nodded toward the front doors.

"You'll get along just fine with Jade. She's about your age and she helps me run the library most of the time.

She's in the children's section re-shelving some books. Why don't you run along and introduce yourself? I'll show Monty around and you and Jade can meet up with us in the recreation room in an hour."

"Yeah, kid. Get a move on, do your job." Monty tossed my camera back at me and shooed me off. This was surprising, considering he always acted very professional and courteous. He would've never spoken to me like that in front of a client. Ms. Freestone was making him act all sorts of weird and I couldn't help but find it a bit funny, something to make fun of later on at the hotel.

Leaving the love birds behind me to continue their battle of the flirts, I headed up the front steps toward the cavern that was the doorway. It almost looked like a mouth of a beast and another set of chills ran down my spine. I swallowed the spookiness I was feeling and pushed myself through the doorway. It was almost like I was walking through a force field. A palpable thickness hung in the air and for a moment my breath caught in my throat, as if something were slowly wrapping its hands around my neck.

I knew this place had its fair share of hauntings, but I didn't think it would be this strong. If it got worse, I would have to beg Monty to pull out of this gig, I was not about to go through what happened in Texas again.

The air inside of the building was indeed thick and icy, almost like one of the first jobs we ever had. It was a church in California that had a ghost inside and what the people failed to tell us was that there was no actual ghost, it was something stronger. I don't remember much, considering within the first few hours of being in the church I'd been knocked out cold. If I had enough sense, I'd turn and run. But I'd be snatched by Monty and tossed right back into this place.

Something was telling me that we had made a grave mistake. There was something about this place that didn't want us here and it was strong. I could smell it, like burnt paper and sour milk. I just hoped who or whatever it was would be able to be asked nicely to leave.

As I stepped onto an ancient looking carpet, the entire library lit up right before my eyes. The creepy feeling I'd had vanished and was quickly replaced with wonder and excitement. I'd never seen so many books before and I was impressed beyond belief. The circulation desk was shaped like a dome but seemed to be void of any other librarians. Where was everyone?

I looked around me in amazement, walls covered in books, statues of famous book characters at the end of the aisles, and large burgundy chairs, perfect for reading were spread out on the dark hardwood floors. I had to crane my neck to get a good look at the second floor which was blocked off by a railed balcony.

I looked up at the ceiling and was prepared to be dazzled by the chandelier I'd seen in research photos, but instead I was underwhelmed. There was a mural painted on the ceiling instead, but it was more boring than exciting or epic. Intricate silver swirls and sharp jagged lines were painted in the middle, almost making me dizzy, and around it balls of light and storm clouds garnished the rest of the mural. Directly in the center of the swirls, was a stark white pentagram with rune signs integrated into the design. Though it was nothing amazing, the feeling I got from it was dark and sinister. I wondered if the last owner had it done after removing the chandelier. Either way it was dreadful.

I lifted my camera up the mural and snapped a quick photo, but when I looked back at it on the display screen, it looked ruined. Something surely didn't want me taking pictures of it.

I turned around and was met with the stained glass windows that I was looking at from outside. The windows had been widened somehow and were now reading nooks, fit with various colored throw pillows and cushions. I took a step forward, toward the window I had seen the girl in and stopped dead in my tracks. All the tiny hairs stood up on the back of my neck. Someone was behind me.

CHAPTER 2:

I SEE DEAD PEOPLE... & BOOKS.

I spun around, nearly tripping on the carpet and was met with the face of a girl, but this one was very much *alive*. She looked to be around my age. I couldn't help that I was a bit disappointed. I really wanted to talk to the ghost girl before Monty and I made any serious commitments to this place.

"Hi, I'm Jade." the girl said. I could only assume that this was the girl who I was supposed to meet in the children's section. Had I really been standing in the library's foyer for *that* long?

"Hi, my name is Simon." I said back. I wasn't good with other people my age. I didn't have any friends to begin with, so conversing with someone brand new to me would be a very interesting yet excruciating experience for sure.

"Are you looking for anything particular?" she smiled, a full set of stark white teeth glaring back at me. She had short curly black hair that hung in spiraled tendrils that ended at the bottom of her ears and she was wearing a filthy green smock.

"I'm actually here with my Uncle. He's the Ghost Expeller." I nearly busted out laughing calling him that. But it was what he forced me to call him.

"Oh, so you're his assistant. Cool. Well, good luck trying to get rid of any of the spirits. You're not the first agency we've had in here in the past few years."

Few years? How many had they called? And all of them failed? This is was definitely way more interesting than finding the ghost girl right now.

"Who was the last?" I asked, hoping it wasn't someone that my uncle hated. Otherwise we'd for sure have to do this job right, so he could rub it in someone's face for a few years.

"Scarlet and Damon Price." she crossed her arms and lifted an eyebrow, as if she were gloating about having an infamous mother and son team of phony Mediums at the library. But I was about to burst her bubble.

"You do know that they're frauds, right? At least

Scarlet is. I know real Mediums when I see them and Scarlet is fake. You wasted your money." I crossed my arms to emphasize my explanation.

The girl's face turned ruby red and she knocked a loose curl out of her vision.

"How would you know a real medium? *Unless you are one.*" Oh crap. I must've been so into outing a fake Ghost Talker that I nearly ousted myself in the process. Monty was going to kill me. I shook the uneasiness from me, hoping that she couldn't see past the worry on my face.

"My uncle is one and I've been with him since I was eight so trust me, I'd know." I was actually quite proud of myself for that explanation I'd just thrown together.

"I see. I've been helping Ms. Freestone out since I was little. My mom used to come in here all the time before she died and she was best friends with Ms. Freestone. This is like a second home to me." A feeling of grief and sadness rushed over me. She'd lost someone too and it still hurt, which I could relate to all too well.

"I'm sorry about your mom," I said, trying to work a smile onto my face.

"Thanks," she smiled and looked down at my camera hanging from my neck. "What's that for?"

"I like taking photos," I replied happily. No one had ever asked why I lugged a camera around from my neck and the fact that someone my age was holding a full conversation with me was astounding.

"Can I see?" Instead of replying, I pulled the strap over my head and handed the camera to her, setting it up so she could just click to the next file.

I watched her eyes widen and her mouth fall open at a few photos. No one ever had taken an interest in my photos, especially Monty. So having a stranger react so incredibly to pictures that I had taken was making me feel a lot better about being in this haunted library.

"How are you able to get such good pics of spirits? Some people spend their whole lives trying to get good ones like these." I watched as she kept clicking through my collection. I couldn't possibly tell her that it had a lot to do with the fact that I was a Ghost Talker. My energy, for some reason, makes them show up almost perfectly in my photos.

"To be honest, I don't know." She was finally going through the ones I'd taken of the front of the library, when the widened smile fell from her face. She was looking at the photo of the ghost girl in the window.

"You... you saw her?" she looked away from my camera's display screen and directly at me. Our eyes locked. Worry filled the space between us.

"I did. I was trying to find her earlier but-"

"-Don't go looking for her. For as long as you're in this library, don't go looking for that girl. You'll regret it." the look in her eyes was grim.

"Why?" I asked.

"Because she's one of the *bad* ones," she swallowed hard and looked around, as if making sure the ghost girl wasn't around to hear her. Something about the way she spoke sent chills down my back once again. She was serious and though it rarely happened, what she said, freaked me out a bit.

She handed my camera back to me and looked around again, nervously twisting her fingers. She was definitely scared of something.

"So are there are *good* ones in here?" I fitted the

strap back over my head and turned off my camera. She looked back into my eyes and nodded.

"Only about three that I know of. Follow me and I'll see if I can get at least one of them to show themselves. It rarely happens for me, but maybe you being here will change things." She spun back on her heels and led the way toward the back of the library. "They don't like pictures, so put that thing away for now."

She gave me a true commanding librarian look and I hastily pulled the strap back over my head. Disappointed, I put my camera into my bag, but left it on video so it could record anything interesting I could use to help Uncle Monty with his so-called "investigation".

It wasn't until we were halfway passed the circulation dome that an eerie voice, sounding ragged and full of static whispered in my left ear.

"*Be careful what you check out...*"

CHAPTER 3:

SERIOUSLY SPOOKED

We'd been walking for what felt like forever, passing a gigantic Fantasy section with a statue of Merlin, the wizard on a pedestal made of copper books. Further down a group of tables had been pushed together with a giant chess board sitting in the middle of them. The pawns were as large as a house cat.

For as long as we'd been walking, I didn't see anyone dead or alive. I could hear a voice or two, one in a different language and another whispering so fast that it almost sounded like a different language. They could've been spirits who didn't want to manifest, or echoes of lost souls passing through. It was hard to tell sometimes.

Deeper inside of the library, I wondered just how many books were in the massive building. The New York Public Library had nothing on this place that went on forever.

After a few more minutes of being silent as we

walked deeper and deeper into the library, I cleared my throat to get Jade's attention. She turned back to me and waited for me to catch up with her.

"Where is everyone? The patrons, the other librarians?" I asked. It was a weekday afternoon and usually libraries are crowded by this time of day from my experience. I'd been in a lot of libraries to know.

"Ms. Freestone is the head librarian, so she closed the library for a week. It will reopen next Monday. She just didn't want any interference or anyone going to spill the beans to the Mayor about what she's trying to do. Besides, not many people come in anymore anyway. Even though our town is famous for this library, not many town's people want to be inside of it, but it's whatever."

She may not have wanted me to see that she cared so much for the library, but I could tell, it was a part of my gift. Sometimes people's emotions get mixed up in the paranormal atmosphere and I hate it. I personally wouldn't want anyone to know how I was feeling. But Jade was so open, she was literally spilling out into the atmosphere and I couldn't ignore it. It bothered her that no one came in here and that she probably fixed up the children's section all the time for nothing, that's what her dirty smock was for. She'd been dusting the shelves. I felt bad for her.

"That sucks," I said. I didn't know how to carry on conversations after being dumped with emotional baggage. I almost wanted to tell her that it would be okay, but then she'd figure out I was a Ghost Talker and I really didn't feel like suffering the wrath of my uncle tonight.

"It does. Well, here we are!" she turned down an aisle of the Science Fiction section. At the end of the aisle was a window and a skinny metal spiral staircase that spun up toward the second floor of the library. Gloomy sunlight was pouring through the window and I could sense that there was someone there. Without realizing it, I took my camera out, turned it to camera mode and snapped a quick photo of the stairwell.

"Didn't I tell you to put that away," Jade slugged me in the arm.

"I'm sorry, it's just reflexes and besides, I got something." I stared down at the display screen. Hovering in front of the window and staircase was a cloud of spirit fog (used only if they don't want to be fully seen or can't manifest correctly.) and if you looked close enough you could see two hands reaching out from it.

I handed my camera to Jade and she looked over the

photo. She looked back and forth to the screen and the stairwell and a nugget of a smile grew on her face.

"For as long as I've helped out in this library, this is one of the ghosts I've never actually seen. I just hear him from time to time, he's very talkative." Jade handed the camera back to me and chewed on her lip for a little bit, as if she were trying to think of something to say.

"What?" I asked, turning off my camera.

"I've only ever seen three ghosts in this library out of the many that haunt it. That creepy girl you took a pic of at the window, the Lady in White on the second floor, and... *Black Veil*, that's what we call her. She's dressed for a funeral and you can never see her face behind the veil she wears. She's the worst of them all. She almost strangled Ms. Freestone a few months ago because we let another agency in." Jade was twisting her fingers and looking out from the corners of her eyes, afraid that Black Veil was near.

"That's pretty intense," I said, turning back to the ghost fog. I'd seen my fair share of the malevolent spirits. One almost threw me out of a third story window when I was nine. I was surprised Jade still hung out here.

"It sure is. There are a lot of them here, I'm sure your uncle will find out soon enough." She stopped twisting her fingers and smiled at me. "That's a great pic, by the way." I could tell that she wanted me to keep taking pictures, but she was too nervous to ask.

"I'll keep taking pictures, if you want," I said, turning on my camera once again and slinging the strap over my head.

"Sure, yeah, I mean, that's fine." She smiled and turned back toward the staircase. "I'm pretty sure that fog is Victor Anders. He haunts this aisle because he used to write books like this before he died. You can hear him from time to time, or throwing books at people who come and sit on the staircase and play on their phones. He hates technology."

I let out a psychic *hello* and it echoed through my head and down the aisle. Jade couldn't hear it, of course, but the spirit could. It was how I tried to get their attention and talk them into not blowing my cover to appear normal.

I waited for a moment and repeated myself. I could only do it twice before it began to drain the energy from my body and I passed out. There was still no answer. For a talkative spirit, this ghost obviously didn't want to talk to me.

"I thought he'd do something, at least throw a book. Oh well, let's go and see if Ms. Freestone and your uncle are waiting for us in the front. She probably wants to start the investigation before the sun goes down, after that it's best that we all leave the building." Jade turned on her heels and began walking back toward the front of the library. Why would we have to leave before the sun goes down?

"What happens after dark?" I asked, trying to catch up with her, my camera swinging back and forth onto my chest. I could feel a bruise coming on.

She kept walking faster but I couldn't keep up with her, so I ran and pulled her to a stop. Her sneakers skidded on the hardwood and let out a screech that echoed around us. It took her a moment to gather up the strength and look me in the eyes. What the heck was going on here?

"That's the thing Ms. Freestone forgot to mention to your uncle. You see, for some reason the paranormal energy is heightened times one hundred in the building after dark. That's when people get killed. At least that's what happened to Mary Summers and Jordan Lopez a couple of months ago." A lump formed in my throat. The librarian and research hadn't mentioned anything about deaths *that* recent. No wonder Ms. Freestone wanted everything under wraps and wanted us here as soon as possible. The ghosts were still killing people.

"That's a very serious thing to forget to mention." I could feel my anxiety simmering beneath my skin. If we'd known about how strong this paranormal activity was, we wouldn't have come. Even if I think my uncle doesn't give two squats about me, he wouldn't want me dead. I'm his money maker.

"No one else wanted to come," Jade finally said, twisting her fingers once again, worrying whether or not Ms. Freestone was going to kill her for opening her mouth. I needed to stop doing that, it felt intrusive.

"I'll talk to my uncle about it," I said and before we could take another step toward the front of the library, a full apparition decided to say hello.

Jade stumbled backward nearly colliding on the ground. This was probably another one of the ghosts she'd never seen before. I stared at him, the temperature around us dropping so low my teeth began to chatter. He was a strong one. But this was not how it was supposed to go. I couldn't work a spirit in front of Jade. This was going to ruin everything.

The spirit was a young boy, maybe around seven or eight and he was carrying a metal train that began to glow brighter than he was. That meant that that he was either growing nervous or getting angry. I took a step back and braced myself. I psychically projected my voice to him. I had to get him to listen to me before he blew my "normal" cover to Jade.

Hi, my name is Simon, I could hear the soft echo of my voice carrying itself over toward the ghost. The boy's ears perked and his eyes grew wide and alert. I could see a giant bloody dent on the side of his head, it was more than likely how he died.

You're not supposed to be here, bad things are gonna happen soon and you need to go, the boy's voice was cold like ice and pierced my brain like a needle. He was strong, *too* strong. I clasped my hands over my head and gritted my teeth.

"Simon, are you okay?" Jade's voice echoed in my head. No! This little boy was blowing my cover. I couldn't let this happen, I had to keep focus.

"Please, stop. I need you to listen to me-" I didn't

realize that I was now talking aloud and Jade could hear everything. I was screwed.

No. You listen. GET. OUT. NOW, as the boy's voice echoed in my head, a rush of cool wind sliced right through us and knocked us both to the ground. The little boy hugged his toy train to his chest, brandished a devilish smirk and evaporated into a soft blue mist.

The wind died in an instant as a few books toppled to the ground beside us. Jade turned to me, a severe look of anger on her face. She didn't even know me enough to be this angry at me, but it hurt all the same.

"What's going on?" Jade snapped. "What are you *really* doing here?"

"I..." I wanted to lie, to find a tall tale to whip up for her to latch onto. But there was nothing left but the truth.

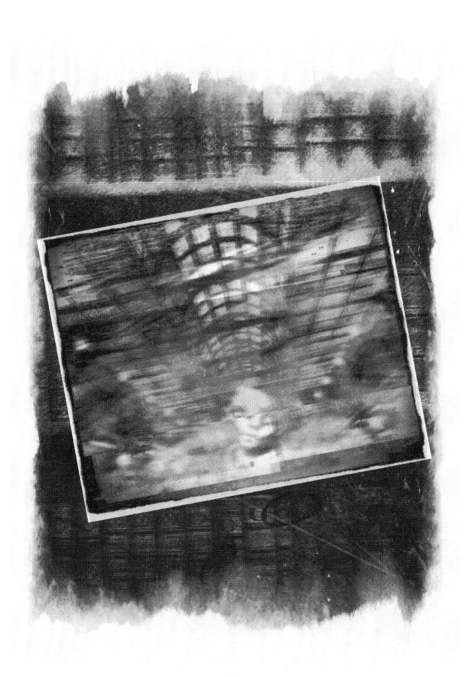

CHAPTER 4:
CAN YOU KEEP A SECRET?

Everything up until this point was going smoothly. I mean, yeah I found out that this place was full to the brim with incredibly strong spirits and I almost got froze to death by a ghost, but my cover wasn't blown... *until now*. Monty was going to kill me. But at least if he killed me here, I would be surrounded by books for the rest of my afterlife.

I looked up from my sneakers and tried to look Jade in the face again. But her glare was so severe, I wouldn't put it past her to be able to kill me with one look.

"Are you just going to stand here silently forever? I want the truth, Simon... or I'll tell Ms. Freestone that we're being swindled once again and maybe this time she'll call the police. Who knows?" Jade was making me nervous and I could feel sweat running down the back of my neck. If she wanted to be a police officer or detective when she grew up, she was sure the best type for that kind of work.

I took in a few deep breaths before pulling her into

one of the aisles and letting the words flood out from my trembling mouth.

When I was done telling her everything, she didn't look angry anymore, in fact she looked like she actually felt sorry for me, which was worse. I hated pity.

"Why do you let him do this to you?" Now she was acting like a therapist. This girl could take over the world if she wanted to.

"I don't have a choice. If I out him, he'll throw me out on the streets or I'll end up in a wayward home and I don't want that. I'd rather help him get rid of ghosts until I'm eighteen than sit in a wayward home waiting until I lost my freaking mind." I couldn't believe I was spilling my entire self to this girl. I barely knew her and she was probably going to tell on me anyway, so what was the point of showing an ounce of vulnerability?

She let out a gigantic sigh that echoed down the aisle and glared at me. She wasn't going to ruin everything after all.

"Fine, I won't say anything. You're young and not to be mean but how in the world are you going to get rid of all of these ghosts?" Jade was right. I knew my strengths and knew that this job was too big for me, but that wouldn't change anything. Monty was not going to budge, I was stuck.

"I have no idea," I said leaning against the shelf, suddenly I was exhausted from using my gift and I just wanted to plop myself on my bed back at the hotel and sleep for a hundred years, at least.

CHAPTER 5:
THE RETURNING

The next day Monty and I were sitting in his car pigging out on greasy burgers before we headed back inside of the library once again. I didn't want to go back inside. I really wanted to help Jade and the library, but a part of me wanted to get as far away from this town as possible. But I knew Monty wasn't going to let that happen.

"I don't like this place," I said swallowing a chunk of burger. All night back at the hotel I tossed and turned, trying to figure a way out of this insanity, but nothing seemed to click.

Monty groaned and took a big slurp of his diet coke.

"Listen kid, this place is making me some big money and what is my favorite thing in the entire world?" Monty nudged me hard. He was trying to play around with me, even though he was terrible at it. But I'd rather have a weird playful Monty than the evil uncle version of him. Some days it was like he didn't even know who he was.

"*Money*," I forced a smile on my face. "But..."

"-No buts! I make the decisions around here and we're staying. Just go around the library and ask the ghosts to shut up instead of telling them to get the heck out. Then *we* can get the heck out of here." I could tell that if I pressed any further, the ugly version of him would make a grand appearance and I wasn't in the mood to deal with that. Sometimes I could see my real uncle in him, as if the real Montoya Santiago was scratching at the door trying to find his way out. But then he'd say something horrible and we'd be right back to mortal enemies.

"Fine," I said, taking a big bite of my burger. I decided to drop the subject, for now.

An hour later Monty was with Ms. Freestone placing his red post-it notes on the areas with the most energy, which was something I had to teach him so people would think he was more legit. I, on the other hand was with Jade in the children's section on the second floor of the library. She was shelving some returns and looked more worried than I'd seen her yesterday.

"Everything okay?" I asked then wanted to slap myself. Of course everything wasn't okay. This freaking

46

library was basically ruining her life.

Jade stood up from shelving a few board books on the bottom shelf and dusted her hands off on her smock.

"I found an old photograph yesterday after you left. It was on one of the tables as if someone had put it there for me to find." I watched as Jade pulled what looked like a postcard out of her back pocket and handed it to me.

Even before I touched it, I knew it was real. I could practically see the paranormal energy oozing out of the photograph. Taking it from her, I turned the photo around and had to squint my eyes to get a perfect look at it.

"What is it?" I asked, staring down at the black and white photograph in my hand. It was sizzling with energy and if I held it any longer it was going to drain me dry.

"I'm pretty sure it's a photo of Black Veil," she explained pointing to a nearly transparent black shape hovering in the photo. I could see it now and it made me shiver.

"This has a lot of dark energy in it, we need to be more careful when handling supernatural objects like this," I said, handing the photo back to her. Instead of putting it back into her pocket she picked up a copy of Peter Pan, slipped the photo into a random part and sat it down on her cart.

I walked away from her and over to the second floor railing. I leaned over and stared down at the first floor. The library looked so much bigger from up high.

"Don't do that!" Jade grabbed me by the arm and yanked me away from the railing. "They could push you over. It's happened a few times."

Chills spun down my spine as I recalled the articles I'd read online.

"So, now that you're back, should I show you around the library more and see if we can talk to some more ghosts?" It occurred to me that maybe she needed to keep her mind off of her life always being in danger, so I smiled back and told her to lead the way.

We were in the back of the second floor where large stained glass windows let in the gray daylight. I could see dust particles floating in the shards of light and for the first time in the building, I got a sense of warmth, which told me that a less harmful spirit was nearby.

I was about to tell Jade that there was someone else back here with us, when a floating orb caught my attention. I watched as it hovered in the air and back through the wooden archway we'd just come through. It hovered for a few seconds more and then vanished behind a dark bookshelf.

Simon... a playful voice slipped into my head. It was young and broken up like a radio station going in and out of tune. I knew it was coming from the dark bookshelf and it didn't want Jade to know it was there.

I turned to Jade, who was looking through her phone's camera, trying to catch something. I admired her for trying, even though there was a good chance she wouldn't get anything without an ability like mine.

"Jade!" another voice rang out and Jade nearly dropped her phone in surprise. "Can you come down here please? I need your help with the basement door again!" I recognized it as Ms. Freestone.

Jade turned back to me and shoved her phone into her smock's pocket, clearly irritated that she had to go and help Ms. Freestone when she'd rather be up here hunting for ghosts.

"I'll be right back. Just stay here and wait for me," Jade said as she spun on her heels and started back through the archway.

"I'll be here," I waved, a little too excited that she was leaving. I watched her as she hurried back to the front of the second floor and waited until I could hear her footsteps charge down the staircase.

It was like fate. The spirit wanted me alone and now it was getting its wish. I didn't know if that was a good thing or a *bad* thing.

The silence on the second floor was almost too much for me, I almost thought I went deaf for a moment as I stood there waiting for whatever spirit who wanted to talk to me to show itself. I just hoped that the warmth I'd felt was the orb I'd seen hide behind that shelf. If not, and it was something horrible, I had to make sure I was ready to run.

Finally to get the ball rolling, as Monty likes to say, I spoke to it.

"Okay," I said aloud. "I'm alone."

As if responding to my voice, a freezing gust of wind fluttered through the heavy velvet curtains on the windows and rushed right into me. I toppled to the ground on my back as a sharp pain erupted in my tailbone. I looked up thinking there'd be nothing there, but of course, I was wrong.

Standing a few feet from me was the same little boy Jade and I had seen yesterday. I crawled backwards instantly afraid of what he was going to do to me.

"Why... are you... afraid of me?" the little boy said. I stopped myself from crawling and looked him in his milky white eyes. He looked hurt, like me trying to get away from him was hurting his feelings.

"You almost hurt us yesterday," I told him, trying not to anger him. My teeth began to chatter from the cold he'd once again brought with him.

"Not *hurt* you..." the boy explained as he took a few steps backward as if I was scaring him now. " *Warn* you..."

"Okay, I'm sorry." I told him trying to calm him down. He seemed to get what I was saying and hugged his toy train.

"Why do you... want to be here?" the boy's voice was gaining more static, as if he were growing weaker. If I wanted to speak to him more, I needed to hurry before he disappeared altogether.

"I'm trying to help you," I said. "How... how did you die?" another gust of freezing wind raked at my body. I forgot how touchy the "*how did you die?*" question was.

The boy hugged his train tighter and stared at me, his wide milky eyes boring into mine.

"Came with mommy to look at books... woman in black pushed me over there," the little boy pointed to the second floor's railing.

"I'm sorry," I told him. 'Woman in black' must've been Black Veil. It seemed she'd been here a really long time.

"I died... you will die too... if you stay longer. She will get you, she... *will.*" His voice began to grow with so much static and he began to flicker like a candle flame.

"What's going on?" I asked him as he hugged his train and closed his eyes tight.

"Gotta go now... she's close by. Bye-bye." And just like that, the little boy was gone. I could still feel the cold and my heart was resting in my throat. As the coldness dissolved, a sudden warmth enveloped me and pulled me toward a wooden coffee table in the second floor's seating area.

Dust covered the table and before I could turn and walk away, a heart began to appear directly in the middle of the dust. I stared at it, wondering why a spirit would show me something like this. Just as quickly as the warmth took me over, the drawing vanished. I spun around to see if I could catch a glimpse of anything leaving, but all I could see was Jade standing in the archway with a look of concern on her face.

CHAPTER 6:
UNCLE MONTY VS SPIDER WEB

I was in the employee break room sipping on a cup of coffee while Monty groaned in exaggerated agony. He was lying on the lunch table while Ms. Freestone wrapped his left wrist with white gauze. While I was having a conversation with the little boy on the second floor, Monty had walked into a spider web. Thinking it was a ghost, he tried to fight it off and ended up tumbling down the basement stairs.

Jade had come up to get me thinking something serious had happened to Monty, but I knew just as I walked into the break room, he hadn't broken anything serious. It was just a sprained wrist and he was playing it up, as usual.

"I'm sorry this happened to your uncle," Ms. Freestone smiled at me, still wrapping gauze around his wrist.

"He'll be fine, right Uncle Monty?" I patted his back, harder than anyone should and he coughed up a grunt, knowing that I knew exactly what he was doing.

"Yeah..." Monty glowered at me. "I'll be fine."

"Good, well I need to get some paperclips to hold that gauze so I'll be right back. I also have to make a quick phone call to make sure the other mediums are going to show. Jade, please go begin locking up for me."

Other mediums? She didn't say anything to us before about having more mediums in the library with us. I waited for Ms. Freestone and Jade to leave before I sat my mug of coffee down, crossed my arms, and stared at Monty.

"Don't look at me like that," he snapped. "I did fall."

"I know you did, but if this some kind of ruse to get more money from Ms. Freestone I think you're a certified butthead, Monty. And how are you going to keep up your so-called ability when the other mediums get here. They'll know."

"I'll figure that out. Just mind your own business, kid." Monty stuck his tongue out at me like a two-year-old and went back to hugging his wrist.

"I saw another ghost earlier. It said we'd be dead if

we stayed much longer," I explained to him. He rolled his eyes and turned to me. But instead of spewing out a load of ignorant fury, he actually looked serious.

"We... we need the money, Simon. The place in NY is gone. They evicted me two months ago. We're basically homeless." Monty explained. I'd never really heard him talk to me like this before. As if he realized that he was speaking to me like a human being, his demeanor took a complete 180 and he snarled at me. "Quit busting my chops, kid."

We were homeless. All of my stuff, all of my belongings from when I moved in with Monty were gone. My dad's key collection, my lucky teddy bear... my mom's favorite VHS tape full of I Love Lucy episodes. It was all gone.

I had to fight back tears as I pushed myself up from the stool I was sitting on and headed out of the room, ignoring Monty. I wanted to hit him. I wanted to punch him so hard in the face that he'd forget who he was. I wanted to get the heck out of here, now.

I hurried down the hallway and headed for the front entrance. Before I could make it to the doors, a hand wrapped itself around my shoulder and pulled me back. I turned to see Jade and the look on her face told me she'd been listening to Monty and me. I wanted to scream.

"You heard everything?" I asked.

"I was about to walk back into the break room when I heard you both talking. It seemed important, so I waited. I'm sorry about everything. Why didn't you tell me about seeing the little boy again?" Now it was Jade who looked somewhat hurt. I had to come up with something. I couldn't tell her the truth. If I did, she'd feel even more at fault than she did right now about me being here.

"I didn't have time... you came up right after he left and told me Monty fell." I could see she believed me and went right back to smiling.

"You were leaving weren't you?" she asked, twisting her fingers.

This time, I couldn't lie.

"I was. I was going to run. I don't know where I was going to go, but I was going to leave Monty-"

"-And *me* behind... I still need your help, Simon."

"I'm sorry," I said and I meant it.

58

"I forgive you," she grabbed me by the arm again and pulled me toward the back of the library. "I found something while I was locking up the back of the library. I wanted to show you."

I followed along, Jade's cool grip leading me down an aisle of extremely old looking books. We stopped in front of a giant yellow book with the number 12 printed on the spine. I tilted my head in wonder as I saw what Jade had found.

"Ectoplasm... *in a book*?" I shook my head. "I've never heard or seen anything like this before." I reached out to touch it and it shocked me, which I should've known would happen. Unless it's coming out of your own body via spiritual possession, ectoplasm is harmful to Ghost Talkers on the outside. The milky white substance was dripping out from the spine of the book, creating a large puddle on the ground before our feet.

"I knew it was something paranormal," Jade got excited. "What is it, exactly?"

"It's a substance of spiritual energy and it basically means there's a lot of energy in this library, which isn't hard to deduce. This book must have some kind of spirit inside of it, which can happen sometimes. They can possess anything from dolls, phones, cameras, to books."

"Is it supposed to stink?" Jade asked as she pinched her nose.

"Yup, like rotten meat and those exploding fart bags. It's gross." Quickly, I pulled out my camera and snapped a photo of the ectoplasm seeping out of the book.

"Um, Simon?" Jade's voice quivered. I tore my eyes away from the ectoplasm and followed Jade's gaze to the window at the end of the aisle. The window was fogged up and in perfect cursive, words began to appear on the glass.

Second floor.

Finally, someone else wanted to talk. I was about to tell Jade we were headed to the second floor again when a familiar voice ripped me out of my thoughts.

"Simon, where are you?" Monty hollered in a playful tone. He was a good actor, I could tell you that.

"Ms. Freestone is probably going to ask you both to come back tomorrow afternoon since the sun's about to go down. Tomorrow we'll see what's waiting for us on the second floor, okay?" Jade whispered as the footsteps of my uncle and Ms. Freestone grew closer and closer.

"Okay," I said and we turned back one final time to the window. The message was gone.

CHAPTER 7:
BLOOD BATH

The next morning at the hotel my mind was still spinning. When we left the library for the second time, I felt like a giant weight had been lifted from my shoulders and even though I wanted to help Jade and the library, a part of me didn't want to step into that place ever again. But I knew that was never going to happen. Ms. Freestone called super early this morning and Monty was about to curse her out for waking him up, if he hadn't recognized her voice first. She told him that she wanted us to come back tomorrow instead. It was like music to my dear uncle's ears.

Since we didn't have to go back to the library until tomorrow, he was out blowing his new check on god knows what. Ms. Freestone gave him half the payment yesterday and after we 'get rid' of the ghosts, she'd give him the last half. He left me here to do a bit more research. He didn't want to hear any more of my thoughts on not going back to the library. He simply just didn't care, his mind was on money as usual.

But I cared and doing further online research wasn't going to help. I needed to get info from the best source in the world, *this* town. I asked Monty if I could explore the town a bit while he was gone, but all I got was a hand wave and a door closed on my face, which in Monty language meant 'whatever'.

I stared at the hotel TV. A news anchor woman with pink hair was talking about a total lunar eclipse happening on Thursday, which was tomorrow. A commercial for a keychain pooper scooper came on and I switched the TV off and jumped up from the bed.

The sun was hidden behind the clouds and it looked pretty windy from the hotel room's bay window. I watched as a couple shuffled past, covering their faces with a shopping bag. Across the street sat a few shops and a restaurant called Johnny's Ribs, which I could smell from inside the hotel room and it was making me hungry.

One of the shops caught my eye as I was about to close the curtain and get ready to head out. The shop was smaller than the rest but had one of the best signs I'd ever seen. It was a wooden sign shaped like a stereotypical ghost and in squiggly blood red letters it read: Ghost Town Souvenirs. The internet research I'd done was right. There was a gift/souvenir shop for the town's own folklore.

I decided that instead of running around the entire town in this crazy weather, I'd hit up that shop and see if the owner or whoever was working could help me out instead. It was worth the walk and even though my life was dedicated to the supernatural, I still enjoyed stuff like that shop from time to time.

Finally after staring for what felt like eternity, I closed the curtain and headed to the bathroom, a towel hanging over my shoulder. We'd been on the road for so long that I figured it was time for a fresh shower.

Flipping the switch on, I tossed the towel on the sink and turned the water on. The bathtub in this room was pretty huge and even had a therapy mode, where the water comes out of these tubes and massages your back for you, pretty sweet. I had to make a mental note to try that out before we checked out of this place.

I was about to pull my shirt over my head when I heard someone call my name.

"*Simon...*" the voice ripped through the air. It was more of a whisper than a call, and it sounded like a girl.

I put my shirt back on, angry that I couldn't even get

naked without a ghost creeping up on me. I wanted to scream, but I knew I'd make whatever it was just as angry as me.

"*Hello!*" I called out, checking the mirror. It happens a lot in horror movies, but in real life mirrors are a gateway to the other side and spirits love to use them when one is near. This mirror was empty.

"*Simon...*" the voice rang out again, louder this time. "*Why didn't you listen to me?*" anger rippled through her voice and the lights above the sink flickered and sizzled.

"*Listen to you...* I don't even know who you are!" I yelled out. I was tired of playing games.

The bathroom door slammed behind me, the wood groaning as if someone was holding it shut. What in the heck!

"Hey! You have no business coming at me like this when I don't even know who you are!" I screamed. I couldn't help that I was getting scared. Yeah, I've dealt with more spirits than anyone would care to count, but that doesn't mean I don't get the creeps sometimes.

"Why didn't you listen to me?" the voice said from

the mirror this time. I swallowed hard and walked back over to the mirror, hoping I wasn't about to have a showdown with an angry spirit.

In the mirror stood a girl, about my height, with long blond hair and a long gaping gash down the middle of her face. Her eyes had been hollowed out and the rest of her face was chapped and corroded like the outside of an old house. Even without eyes, I could see that she was full of rage and at any moment she was going to bust.

Suddenly the bathroom grew colder and I shuddered. Whoever she was, she was strong and I could feel my heartbeat moving toward my throat in fear. I wasn't scared because of how she looked. I'd seen my fair share of grotesque looking spirits, some with their insides hanging out of their outsides, so I was pretty used to seeing some pretty messed up stuff. It was her strength that freaked me out most. Her aura was interesting. She didn't seem evil, she seemed misunderstood, and hurt.

I was trying my best to figure out what she wanted with me, and then it hit me like a freight train: she was the girl in the window from the library. The one Jade told me to stay away from. But in the window she looked different. She didn't have a giant gash on her face in the window, she looked almost peaceful at the library.

67

"You're the girl from the library," I told her, trying to calm her down, but the lights above the sink were still flickering and it was still freezing. It was so cold my arms began to prickle as if a million tiny ants were underneath my skin. I'd never felt like this before.

She glared at me and tried to open her mouth to speak, but it was as if something were forcing it to stay shut. With all her might, she forced her mouth open and the sides of her cheeks split open like a fresh wound. I took a tiny step back. I'd never seen a ghost do something like that before.

Her jaw was now hanging at an awkward angle as she tried to speak.

"*Must... stay... away...*" she said, her tongue slithering in and out of her now broken mouth like a snake. I decided that I wasn't scared of her anymore, I was scared *for* her. Something was doing this to her.

"I tried," I told her. "My uncle won't listen to me!"

"MAKE HIM LISTEN!!" she screamed with so much force that the walls rattled. Her jaw tore away from her face and flew to the ground so she couldn't speak right anymore. I could feel the rage rising in her and I wanted to run, but I couldn't. She was forcing me to stay put. I turned away from her and saw that the bathtub was now full of blood instead of water and it was pouring over the rim of the tub. The floor of the bathroom began to fill with the crimson liquid and the sharp aroma of copper attacked my senses. I hated the smell of blood.

I turned back to the girl and watched as she helplessly writhed in place as if something was attacking her from the inside. Piece by piece parts of her skin flaked away until she was almost bone. I could see the pain in her face and I wanted to stop it. This was one of the worst encounters I'd ever experienced and it was all because of that stupid library.

"WHY DIDN'T YOU LISTEN?" a crying whisper shot through both of my ears like a razor blade and I leaned on the sink from the pain. I pushed myself back up and stared at the girl in the mirror, disintegrating right before my eyes.

"WHO IS DOING THIS TO YOU?" I screamed.

She looked like she was trying to tell me, but something was holding her back. With all her might she let out a scream, louder than I'd ever heard and then erupted into tiny chunks of dust.

Free from her grasp, I collapsed to the ground and into the blood. The thick, coppery liquid filled my mouth and ears as I tried to call out for help. I pushed myself up from the ground and slammed myself against the wall. When I opened my eyes, I realized that it was no longer blood, it was just water, and the bathroom was flooded.

I decided to skip the shower after what happened in the bathroom and had to call the front desk to tell them that the bathroom was flooded. Monty was never going to let me hear the end of it when he found out. Luckily, the woman at the front desk could hear my distraught voice and told me that she'd send someone up to clean it before my uncle got back. I wanted to ask her if she's ever considered adopting a kid, but she hung up before I could say another word.

I was sitting on the bed, my head in my hands trying to figure out what the heck happened in the bathroom. I'd never had a spirit from a haunt follow me back to a hotel, or even home. So the fact that the girl was able to do that and conjure up all that power to cause hallucinations meant that the library was more troubling than I already knew. And not just that, something had come along with her and was making sure she kept her mouth shut.

If I could, I'd run. I'd take some of Monty's not-sosecretly-hidden-in-his-underwear money and take the next bus out of Childermass. But I didn't have that type of courage. I could face ghosts, but real life was a lot more terrifying than an angry spirit or two.

I was going through possible escape scenarios in my head when someone knocked on the room's door. Maybe whoever was sent to clean the bathroom could let me know of the closest bus station. I pushed myself up from the bed and headed to the door, my heart still sitting in my throat like a frightened child.

I pulled the door open, expecting to see a plumber of some kind with a frustrated expression, but instead I was met with a dreadfully familiar face.

CHAPTER 8:
BOOK OF SHADOWS

"Jade," I said. My throat tightened as I pulled the door open the rest of the way and crossed my arms over my soaked chest. This was nowhere near what I had begun to plan and from the look on my face, she could tell that I was not as happy to see her as she was to see me.

"Is this a bad time?" she asked, lugging a giant black book in her arms. She looked as if she were about to fall over from how heavy it seemed.

"Yes," I grunted, still angry that she'd shown up when I was about to make my supposed break for it. I just wanted her to go and never come back.

"Oh." The smile melted from her face and she looked hurt. Staring at her frowning, I began to feel bad. It wasn't her fault that the library was insanely haunted, she was trying to help, and I was being a royal jerk.

"Sorry," I said, letting my arms fall away from my chest. "I just got a visit from one of your library's ghosts and it didn't go well, as you can tell by me being Water Park soaked." I gestured to my damp t-shirt and jeans.

"One of them followed you?" she was smiling as she hurried into the room and I closed the door. She tossed the book on the bed and turned back to me like a kid at story time waiting to hear the ending of a scary story.

"Yeah, the girl in the window I told you about. She wasn't as bad as you said she was. She didn't seem *evil* at all. She was just trying to help."

"That doesn't seem right," Jade said. "She was always throwing books off of shelves at me and locking me in the bathroom with the lights flickering off and on. And she pushed me off of a ladder once and I sprained my ankle. That's pretty evil, in my book."

That kind of stuff is child's play compared to what I've been through. But we were in danger and things needed to be dealt with as soon as possible.

"Someone was trying to stop her from telling me something, and it was ripping her to pieces right in front of me. Whoever it was must be so strong that they could destroy a ghost and that's pretty freaking terrifying. In my opinion, whatever it was that was doing all of that stuff to her, it was from the library too. *It just had to be.*" I could see the fear in Jade's eyes and even though I felt bad telling her that the library was more horrible than she thought, she had to know everything.

"What are we going to do?" Jade looked deflated, as if all the life had been sucked out of her body. She was scared for her life, and I couldn't blame her. She was looking at me with hope and I wanted to turn away and run back into the bathroom.

But something inside of me was not done with the library. I couldn't deny that a part of me wanted to run, but the stronger part of me, wanted to kick some ghostly butt.

"I have to destroy it." the words came out of my mouth and for once they didn't feel wrong, or forced. They felt *right.*

"We, you mean *we* have to destroy it. I'm not letting you do it alone. It was Ms. Freestone that brought you and your uncle to our library and now I'm going to help you do some serious ghost damage- which reminds me!" she turned and pulled the book she'd brought along with her off the bed and plopped it on the ground.

"Why did you bring a bible?" I asked as I got down on the ground and watched Jade pull a buckle free and open the book to a bookmarked page. It looked old, seriously old, and it even smelt like soggy earth.

"It's supposed to look like a bible but it's a book of shadows. I went to the second floor again after you left because I'm super impatient. I know, I suck." She let a giggle escape her as she turned to the next page. "And I found this sitting in a ray of sunlight on the floor and our library doesn't have these types of books in our system. I'm pretty sure a ghost put it there for us."

"So there's more good spirits in that library full of souls after all. That's a great thing, Jade. It means we aren't alone in this. We have someone on the other side and that's the best kind of help there is."

"I think I know *who* it is." Jade said and turned to me. "The Lady in White. She's a ghost who lets me see her sometimes, just fragments though. I've never actually seen her full body. But she's always doing tiny things in the library, like helping patrons by pushing the book they're looking for out of the shelf, or watching over the kids in the children's section when the parents aren't paying attention. She can't talk though. She's always writing things, so I wondered if the writing on the window was her and I guess I was right."

"I guess you were. But what about this Black Veil lady you were talking about. What's her deal?"

Jade looked around before saying anything, as if the ghost followed her here too. I wouldn't be surprised if it did, so I took a survey of the room before putting my focus back on Jade.

"Is she the big bad in the library? Is that why you're so afraid?"

"She is. Truthfully, I don't know just how many spirits are in the library, but like I told you, she's the worst of them all. As I said she wears a black veil so you can't see her face, and she brings this cold front with her wherever she goes and it's not a regular type of paranormal chill, it's icy and prickly as if it's seeping into your skin and laying eggs or something." I wondered if that icy feeling in the bathroom was Black Veil. From what Jade was telling me, it seemed so. But I didn't want to scare her even more so I decided to keep that bit to myself.

I watched the fear build even more on Jade's face as she continued to explain "She has a special kind of hatred for Ms. Freestone though. She almost killed her last summer when an entire bookshelf collapsed and Ms. Freestone missed it by an inch. Just after it happened, I saw Black Veil, standing near the shelf. She's one of the only ones that you can see full body and I'd rather not see her at all, if I'm honest."

I'd heard some pretty insane stuff during most of our cases, but what Jade was telling me seemed seriously intense, almost demonic. And I didn't have a good track record with demons. They really didn't like me. I shuddered thinking about Texas.

"Have you ever thought she might be a demon?" I asked, goose bumps erupting all over me.

"She might be. I never really thought to look into it more. Now, I feel kind of stupid." She rubbed at her arms, embarrassed.

"Don't be, demons are not the kind of entities you mess with. Even researching them can set things off."

"Thanks, I feel a bit better now." Jade smiled as she went back to flipping through the pages. "There's a page in here with that mural above the circulation desk on it. It was saying something about- oh, here it is!"

I looked down at the book and swallowed hard. Right there on the page was a perfect drawing of the mural, almost as if whoever owned this book had painted the mural in the library themselves. On the bottom was a paragraph written in what seemed like blood that Jade began to read out loud:

"*The Déjà Quimorta is a symbol and conduit to the spirit world. First introduced centuries ago by unknown occultists, drawing the symbol on a wall, mirror, or door, opens an instant connection to the spirit world and allows spirits, demons, and other supernatural beings access to the human realm. As long as the symbol is present and active, it feeds great power to the person dead or alive who wields it.*"

"So basically it *can* be stopped," I said.

"If we knew how, yes, it seems so." Jade flipped to the next page but it looked like that was the only page about the mural.

From the way everything looked Jade and I were stuck on this one. How would we figure out how to destroy the symbol without the right help? Who in their right mind would help us with something so *insane*? And then it clicked. It looked like the Ghost Town Souvenir shop was going to be the giant help we needed after all.

CHAPTER 9:

GHOST TOWN SOUVENIRS

The Ghost Town Souvenirs shop was way smaller inside than the outside made it appear. There weren't aisles or even sections, it was just one straight line full of shelves of various trinkets and town souvenirs that led toward the cash register at the very end. It was very anti-climatic, if you asked me.

I stopped in my tracks, staring at a row of mason jars that looked as if they had actual spirit orbs sitting inside. A green tag on the bottom of one of the jars read: *Looking to take a spirit home with you? Grab one of these extraordinary jars complete with an actual ghost inside. Warning: Do not touch or open these jars. You'll live to regret it.*

Now, that was a pretty interesting selling point. There were several jars left and dust rings on the shelf showing that people actually bought some. I picked up one of the jars and stared into it. I could see a mass of what looked a cloud and an orb of blue light inside. I tried looking for a switch or a button, but I couldn't find one. As I held the jar, I could feel the energy that beamed from within. It was real and it almost made me drop it. The memory of that ghost in that jar back in New York appeared in my head.

"What are you doing? You'll make Emerson mad." Jade took the jar from me and carefully put it back on the shelf.

"Who's Emerson?" I asked. Instead of answering Jade took me by the arm and practically dragged me up to the check-out counter.

We stood there for a few seconds staring at an old cuckoo clock that had a ghost waiting behind the number twelve instead of a bird ready to boo instead of hoot. It was almost noon and I only had a couple more hours before I had to be back at the hotel before Monty threw a fit, if he was even back by then.

"Emerson is the owner. He's also the town historian." Jade explained and began banging on a bell that sat near a canister of ghost shaped lollipops.

I heard an irritated grunt and then a giant man, almost the size of a Sasquatch stepped out from a beaded doorway, swinging his arms around, knocking strings of black beads out of his way. When he saw us standing at the counter, the annoyed look on his white bearded face disappeared and was replaced with a wide, welcoming grin.

He looked familiar, like I'd seen him before somewhere, but it wasn't registering with me. Maybe I'd seen him in my research of Childermass Public Library? Yeah, that had to be it. As if sensing my thoughts, he looked away from me and down at Jade.

"Jade Madden! It's been a while since I've seen you. And who might this young fella be? I know everyone and their dog in town and I've never laid eyes on you before." he switched his gaze from Jade to me and pinched one eye shut, trying to peer into me. He was a Ghost Talker too.

My name is Simon Santiago, I projected to him and he took a step back, not anticipating my move.

"Welcome to Ghost Town Souvenirs Simon," the hulking man said aloud and Jade glared at us both.

"What's going on?" Jade crossed her arms.

"He's like me. He can talk to ghosts too." I told her. To be honest I felt a bit more comfortable being around someone like me. It didn't happen as often as I would like it to. It was good to know that there were other people out there like me. It made me feel less alone than I already was.

"So what can I do for you both?" Emerson leaned on the counter and smiled at us.

I didn't know how to do it. How do you just tell someone that there's a portal to the other side just chilling in your local library? It's not as easy as it sounds. I sneaked a peek at Jade and nodded at her to go ahead and do the talking. I wasn't particularly good at explaining things, especially crazy stuff like this.

"It's the library," Jade said. "Ms. Freestone hired Simon and his uncle to get rid of the ghosts and we just found out that it's not as easy is it seemed to be."

"There's too many spirits in that dang building, Jade. Ms. Freestone should know better than to mess with that mass amount of paranormal activity. I don't even know why she still lets you help her run that place, you could get seriously hurt. If I were her, I'd shut the place down and try to open another library in town." He was being blunt, and even though it hurt Jade's feelings, she had to know that he meant it from a good place.

"He's right... but there has to be something we can

do!" I looked up at Emerson. He took a moment and stared off into the shop behind us, thinking.

"There might be something, but without anything to help us, it's useless even talking about it," Emerson looked down at a map of the town that was underneath a layer of glass on the counter.

"We might have something after all," Jade finally said and startled Emerson by slamming the book of shadows onto the counter, a cloud of dust erupting into the air. He looked at the book with wide eyes and pulled it toward him.

" *Yes...* it seems you might."

After several minutes of Jade twisting her fingers and me chewing on my bottom lip while Emerson studied the mural, a pair of wiry glasses perched on the end of his strawberry shaped nose, the big man clapped his hands together in excitement and then turned the book back around to face us.

"This is very dark magic and you two need to understand that before you go any further with this. This mural, I've seen it before and it's one of the most powerful symbols in the world. I'm surprised it hasn't caused a bigger ruckus at the library for being so dang strong."

"We have to stop it," I said, determined. It didn't matter how strong this thing was. We had to make it stop or something big was going to happen eventually and ruin everything this town held dear.

"We understand, Emerson. We just need help. *Please.*" Jade stared at Emerson with a pleading gaze that would probably get her free ice cream for life at Baskin-Robbins.

Finally, Emerson caved and sighed in defeat.

"See, these runes are like keys and if you don't have the key to something..." he looked at us from behind his glasses, waiting for us to finish his sentence.

"Then you can't unlock it," Jade and I said in unison.

"Correct! Which means you'll have to *destroy* the mural somehow and since it's a doorway for the spirit world, you can't just remove the entire mural, you have to have a special spell for it... and I know the perfect person for you to get it from."

WARNING: Do not touch or open these jars. You'll live to regret it.

CHAPTER 10:

MADAME HELENA

I followed Jade through a bundle of trees behind a brick building that was for lease. I couldn't help feeling weird about finding this woman, Madame Helena, who Emerson called a *real* witch. He told us where to go and to tell her that Emerson Lewis sent us. I just hoped that whoever this woman was, she could actually help us. If not, we were definitely screwed.

I pushed a wad of willow tree branches out of the way and nearly tripped over a log as Jade began to walk faster.

"Have you ever met this lady before?" I asked as I caught up with her.

"Nope, this is all news to me. I've grown up here and didn't even know about her. I just hope she can help us," Jade explained as she lugged the book of shadows in her arms.

"Me too," I replied as I pulled a chunky branch out of

the back of my shirt. How much farther did we have to go? But as if it could hear me, a house appeared in the distance across a tiny creek.

The gloomy afternoon sun peered through the gaps in the branches above us as we approached the creek. Jade and I stopped and turned to each other.

"Are you scared?" I asked her. I didn't really *have* to ask, I could feel it. I couldn't deny that I was bit spooked too.

"A little," a smudge of a smile grew on her face and she walked over to a tiny bridge that looked like it was made from Popsicle sticks and couldn't even hold a dog's weight.

I waited for Jade to cross since I couldn't swim. She made her way over in a dash and I put one foot on one plank, feeling like a wuss. Jade looked back and saw me still standing on the other side and couldn't help but let out a tiny chuckle.

"Are you scared?" she tilted her head to the side and smirked.

"*No*," I said and pushed myself onto the bridge and ran across as if the whole bridge were on fire. I tripped at the end and tumbled onto a pile of dead leaves. My right knee was stinging and I didn't have to look down to know that I'd scraped myself pretty bad.

"You'll live," Jade giggled and began to walk toward the house.

"Ha-ha!" I dusted myself off and picked myself up from the ground. Luckily I was wearing a pair of jeans and Jade couldn't see that I'd messed up my knee pretty bad. I made a mental note to clean it up when I got back to the hotel.

I followed Jade up a tiny hill and into the front yard of a rundown looking cottage. Candles of various sizes and colors were burning in the windows, seemingly warding off bad spirits. I could smell incense burning and I got the chills thinking of Texas again.

"You okay?" Jade turned back to me. She was worried about me.

"That smell... it reminds me of something," I said.

"Of what?" Jade probed, leaning forward, wanting to know more. I told myself I'd never bring up what happened in Texas again, but maybe it would bother me less if I told someone. So I looked down at my shoes and told Jade everything.

"When I was nine, Monty took me on a job to El Paso, Texas. Someone had called us about a haunt called The Diamond House. It was a white house that sat on a hill on the corner of a dead street and most of the windows were shaped like diamonds. The two houses on either side of it had been demolished because whatever was happening in that house was affecting the neighbors..."

I took in a deep breath, exhaled, and continued.

"The people who called us didn't tell uncle Monty how *bad* everything was and they forgot to mention that it wasn't a spirit that was haunting The Diamond House... it was a *demon*. We weren't in the house but a half hour before things started getting crazy. The people who brought us there ran out of the house and left me and Monty in there. That was the first time I saw my uncle scared of something..."

I stopped for a moment and caught my breath. Even talking about it was making me feel horrible again. Jade placed a hand on my shoulder.

"It's okay, Simon. Keep going," Jade told me. So I

did.

"Well, we tried to leave but the demon wasn't going to let us. So I tried to tell it to leave me and Monty alone, but that just angered it more. Then it did something I will never forget... it glamoured itself as my parents and started telling me that they didn't love me and that they were happy they were gone because they didn't have to deal with me anymore. Monty saw and heard everything because the demon let him..."

I realized that I was crying and that was new for me. I never really cried and I couldn't remember the last time I had. And now someone I didn't even really know too well was watching me cry like a baby. But I sucked it up and kept going.

"The house was full of candles and incense burning so I kicked a row of candles to the side and the entire living room caught on fire. I don't really know what happened after that. I just know that I woke up in the hospital and Monty told me that I did a good job and then told me we almost got ourselves killed. But I'll never forget any of that. It was the only time I saw my parents after they died and it still messes with me to this day."

"I'm sorry, Simon. But we're going to fix this. I

promise."

"What is it that you want!" a voice startled Jade and I
as we flew back in fright and nearly fell into a puddle of rain
water near the wooden fence that surrounded the house.

Jade composed herself before she spoke.

"Emerson Lewis sent us," Jade squeaked. This
woman was dressed from head to toe in what looked like
scarves sown together. I'd never seen anything like it. She
had stark white short hair and what looked like a thousand
beaded necklaces hung from her withered neck. Her eyes
were so blue I almost expected for them to glow. She
reminded me of the bayou witches from a case Monty and I
had in New Orleans last year.

"Ah, yes. He called me and told me everything. Now,
get inside before all the bad juju out here in these trees
follows you inside my house- and wipe your feet." Jade and I
didn't need to be told twice. We rushed inside as the woman
closed the door behind her. She led us through a curtain of
beads into a room with a large round table covered in tarot
cards and candles, some with saints on the outside.

On the walls were mirrors of all different shapes and
sizes, most covered with black veils. This must've been the

most powerful room in the house. I could just imagine how many ghosts were in these mirrors. The hairs on the back of my neck stood on end as a rush of cool wind came out from one of the mirrors by my jacked up knee.

"Thank you for helping us, Madame Helena," I told the woman.

"You are welcome, young spirit seeker. I can feel your energy. I can taste it, which means it's immense and will do great things. Your bloodline is a good one, Simon Santiago. Don't let the fear of failing ruin you. If you put your soul into it, you will be unstoppable."

"Um, thank you," I said, not really expecting a pep talk from a woman I'd never met before. How did she know so much about me and my bloodline? What else could she tell me?

"That's awesome and all, but we're kind of on a time crunch here." Jade said as she put the book of shadows on the table and flipped to the mural page for the woman.

"I see..." Madame Helena put a hand on the page and began tracing the intricate design of the mural with a broken finger nail.

"We're going back to the library tomorrow and we-" Madame Helena held up and a finger, interrupting me.

"Does insanity run in your family, Simon Santiago?" Madame Helena peered at me like I was an idiot. I didn't understand what I'd done.

"What does that have to do with anything?" Jade piped in, crossing her arms. She was trying to defend me.

"A full lunar eclipse, the *blood moon*, is happening tomorrow night. It would be ludicrous to go into that building during a blood moon when the supernatural activity is at its highest. It's plain suicide, young man."

I hadn't thought about it that way and now I felt like a freaking idiot. I guess insanity does run in my family after all. But then I thought about it for a minute and if it could give that much power to paranormal energy... why couldn't it do the same for a spell?

"Wouldn't the blood moon's energy work just the same for this spell that we need to do?" Madame Helena didn't speak. She stood staring into a mirror, seemingly having a silent conversation with someone inside of it.

Then she turned back to Jade and I and nodded in

95

agreement.

"Yes, it would... but you do understand that you will be putting your lives in complete danger? You could die and end up haunting that library just like all the other spirits for eternity. Think about it."

So I thought about it. I stood there, going through everything in my head: Jade and Ms. Freestone risking their lives every day to keep that library open to the public, Monty not listening to me when he should, me being the only one with the ability to talk to the spirits... and finally that Diamond House demon trying to hurt me.

I was done letting the dead mess with my life. I needed to take control and set things right.

"I understand," I told Madame Helena.

"Me too," Jade chimed in, smiling at me.

"Then I have what you need. I just need to tell you how to use it- Girl, yes, you-" the woman pointed at Jade with a long red nail. "Go into the room with the red door and bring me the purple sack sitting on the table and be quick about it!"

Jade spun on her heels and left the room. Madame Helena and I were alone and I had an eerie feeling that this was *exactly* what she wanted.

The Diamond House
Located in El Paso, TX

CHAPTER 11:
TRUST

"I needed you alone, Simon Santiago. Please don't be frightened, I just need to speak with you, candidly of course. Don't worry about the girl, she'll be stuck in that room until I say so."

Even though she told me not to be frightened, I couldn't help but be a little worried for my life. My heart beat crept up into my throat and felt like it was trying to rip itself out of my neck. I tried to calm myself down, but I just made it worse.

"I'm listening," I told Madame Helena.

"Good. Now, something doesn't *feel* right. The spirits are trying to tell me something, but it's coming in muffled and broken. Who exactly invited you to the library to rid it of these spirits?"

I didn't know where she was going with this, but I

had to find out.

"Octavia Freestone, the head librarian."

Madame Helena pressed her hands into her temples and listened. I tried my best but I couldn't hear anything. Whatever these spirits were telling her, they obviously didn't want me to hear it.

Suddenly the mirrors on the walls began to rattle and glow. I could feel them, all of the spirits in this room, but I couldn't hear or see them for the life of me.

After a few moments of her talking silently to the air, she opened her eyes and stared at me head on.

"Be careful of this woman, this Octavia Freestone. The spirits are telling me that she cannot be trusted... that she did not bring you here under the circumstances of which you were told... and that the girl is in grave danger as well."

"None of this makes sense. Why would she really bring me here?" I tried to think, to decipher what it could be that Ms. Freestone could want from me... but I came up with nothing. And why was Jade in danger?

"The spirits will not tell me... I'm sorry. But if they

are right, then you must be on high alert when entering the library tomorrow evening." Madame Helena released her hands from her temples and nearly collapsed onto the round table in front of her.

"Are you okay?" I hurried up to her and helped her back up. She turned to me and laid both of her hands on my shoulders.

"You must be the one to do the spell. When the entire moon has been draped in darkness, the mural will reflect onto the ground of the library. Then and only then can you erase the runes, with your own blood, of course." My face contorted as I looked at her. "I never said it would be easy, Simon Santiago. And once you've done this... you must get out of that building as fast as your feet can take you... because without the mural, the entire building will come down. *Do you understand?*"

I took in a deep breath, exhaled, and stared into Madame Helena's eyes. I could feel the warmth in her soul. She didn't even know me... but she believed in me.

"Yes, I understand."

CHAPTER 12:

MUMS THE WORD

The whole way back to the hotel, Jade and I were silent. It was mostly because of me. I needed to focus. And I really wanted to tell her about Ms. Freestone, but Madame Helena told me not to. She even told me not tell her the real way to destroy the runes. She couldn't be sure if Ms. Freestone could get into Jade's head and manipulate her. It could ruin everything.

So when she brought Jade back into the room, she made up a spell for us to do, which was the reason why Jade was carrying a purple sack of chalk dust and vile of snake venom. Jade didn't even remember being stuck in that room for so long. It was like it never happened.

I felt bad not telling Jade the truth, but it was for a good reason and I just hoped she forgave me after this was all over with.

We made it to the hotel room door as the sun began to go down and I could hear Monty in the room watching

TV. He was going to give me hell when I walked into that room.

"Well, I guess I'll see you tomorrow," Jade smiled as she heard Monty rooting for something he was watching. "Good luck with *him*."

Jade turned on her heels and began walking down the hall.

"Jade," I called out. She stopped and turned back to me.

"Be careful in the library tomorrow," I told her, forcing a smile onto my face. I just wanted to tell her everything. "We'll be there in the afternoon."

"I'll be alright," she said. She took a look at her phone and then sprinted down the hallway. She was probably late too.

I let myself into the hotel room, bracing myself for the fireworks that were Monty's famous rants. He was sitting on one of the beds with a tub of chocolate ice cream and he was eating it with a waffle. I wouldn't expect anything different from him.

"I'm back," I waved at him and he finally noticed me. He shoved the waffle into the ice cream and placed it on the dresser separating the beds. He turned the TV off and crossed his arms. I was in for it.

"Where the heck have you been? I was worried."

My eyes shot wide open and I glared at him in surprise. *Worried?* He never ever expressed any type of emotion about me other than anger and frustration. So this was new for me. And it kind of scared me.

" *Worried?*" I asked.

"Yeah..." he cleared his throat. "Worried about my money. I don't need you disappearing and stuff. Now get to bed, we got a lot of work to do tomorrow."

I let my shoulders slump as I walked over to my bed and tried to make myself comfortable. I guess he really didn't care about me like I thought. But what was new?

In the silence Monty cleared his throat again.

"And I was *kinda, sorta, maybe* worried about you too. Now go to bed." he clicked the TV on and went back to pigging out on his junk food.

Tears tickled my face as they ran down my cheeks. I needed to hear that, even if it was because he was in a good mood. I needed it. I wanted to turn around and tell him everything. But I wasn't supposed to tell him either and even though it shouldn't have bothered me because it was Monty for crying out loud, it did.

Tomorrow I was either going to live to tell the story about one of the most or probably the most haunted libraries in the world... or by the end of the night, I was going to be hovering through its aisles, tossing books off the shelves, for eternity.

CHAPTER 13:

A LITTLE HELP

We were standing outside of the library again. But this time I didn't want to go in. Just two days ago I was somewhat excited that I'd be inside such a huge library, surrounded by thousands of books. But now, I couldn't wait to get as far away from this place as possible.

Monty nudged me in the shoulder and pointed to the foreboding structure. I looked up and saw Jade waving at us through one of windows. I bet she was surprised to see us back, even though I promised I would be.

"We're making some good money cleaning this dump out. We already got a new job waiting for us in New Jersey. Now, how do I look?" Monty nudged me again and I reluctantly turned to him and pretended to care what he looked like.

"You look good," I said, shrugging my shoulders.

"Just *good?*" he snapped. Now, this was the uncle I

knew.

"Great, awesome, spectacular!" I pushed a laugh out of me.

"Don't get smart with me," he fixed his tie and then for what seemed like the millionth time, tried to slick back that godforsaken cowlick.

The doors to the library flew open and a rush of icy wind spilled down the stone steps and over to us. Monty shivered and that was the first time I'd ever seen him do that in public. I wanted to blurt out everything I was holding in. I wanted to tell him that Octavia might possibly be evil and about the crazy strong mural in the library. I really wanted to tell him how I was going to destroy the mural, all by myself.

Someone cleared their throat and I turned back to the doorway, preparing myself to look Octavia in the face and try to get a good reading out of her. But instead of the mysterious librarian standing on the top step of the entrance, there was a short woman with bright red hair and a pair of square green glasses resting on her nose.

She looked young, maybe a few years older than me and she looked worried, as if something was bothering the heck out of her. I tried to take a peek into her head, but it was as if someone had slammed a door right in my face.

Nice try, squirt. I'm too good for that, she projected at me and winked. In surprise I watched her walk down the rest of the steps toward us, wondering if she was one of the medium's Octavia had talked about.

"I'm Macy Parker," she grabbed Monty's hand and gave it a good shake. "I'm a medium from Los Angeles. Octavia invited me along with several others who are already waiting in the library. We're here to help you out."

I'd completely forgotten about the other mediums possibly being here. Monty and I didn't even get to go over our plan on how to mask his 'normalness' now that she knew I was a Ghost Talker too. Things were about to get much crazier.

"I work alone," Monty snapped.

"Well, we're here now so you're going to have to deal with us. It looks like the paranormal activity in this place is too much for two mediums to take out, so Octavia called us in. Now, follow me. We've got a lot of work to do before this blood moon tonight." Macy turned and headed back up the steps, leaving us behind.

"*More mediums? Blood moon?* What the heck is going on?" Monty turned to me as if I was supposed to know everything. But I couldn't say a word, so I shrugged and sprinted up the steps and into the abyss of hell on earth.

We were all standing in the foyer of the library. Most of the comfy looking chairs had been pulled and organized into a giant circle so we all could take a seat, but none of us wanted to sit down. The psychic energy was massive.

I could feel it in the tips of my fingers and in my bones. It was a good feeling and I didn't want it to stop. I had to admit that I did feel a little better being surrounded by a few other Ghost Talkers. It was a warm feeling in this dark and cold place.

After everyone had introduced themselves, I studied everyone with my own eyes. There was of course, Macy Parker from Los Angeles. Then there was Rick Fuentes from Houston who had one of the most amazing electronic wheelchair's I had ever seen. And lastly there were twins, Jacob and Jessica Lee. They were fourteen and from what I gathered, very expensive and a bit snotty.

Everyone seemed to like each other, expect for Monty who was now sitting in a chair to my right, sulking like a big baby. He was worried about his money and with these new mediums here to help, he didn't know if he'd be paid less or at all anymore.

Someone cleared their throat and we all turned in unison toward two figures heading our way from the back of the library. As they grew closer and came into the afternoon sunlight that was pouring through the windows, I could see that it was Octavia and Jade. Madame Helena's words popped up in my head, *the girl is in grave danger.*

How was I going to keep Jade safe with her around Octavia the entire time? Now that I was looking at Octavia in a different way, I could see how she could appear sweet and kind and still harbor wickedness inside of her. She could have so much power that she could simply be cloaking everything. I'd read books about things like that before. I could feel the anger rising in me and from the looks on the Jacob and Jessica's faces, they could feel my anger too.

"Hello everyone!" Octavia announced as she walked past Monty and greeted the other mediums with handshakes and hugs. "Thank you so much for coming. You see, I thought things would be able to be handled by Mr. Santiago over here and his assistant," she gestured toward my uncle, who was now at attention, smiling.

"But if we all can work together, I'm sure we can take care of everything by sunset."

"I think so too," Macy agreed and Monty scowled at her.

"Now, Jade will assign the areas that are most active to you all with these index cards that we created for you. Do your best to be as polite to the spirits you will be dealing, we don't want anything horrible to happen to anyone. When you've done your best, whether you persuade a spirit to leave in peace or not, we will all meet back here at 5:15pm to go over everything and then you all can go back to your hotel rooms and take a good nap." Everyone, except me, giggled at her words. "And thank you!"

With that, she spun on her heels and walked off toward the back of the library where she came from, the click-clacking of her heels echoing like stray bullets. I watched as she kept sneaking quick glances back at us. I swore I saw a devilish smirk form on her face and I turned away. A chill shot down my spine and I swallowed hard. Things were about to get real, *real* interesting.

CHAPTER 14:
A SECRET LIBRARY

Monty, Jade, and I got the second floor of the library and so did the twins. Monty couldn't have been more irritated and angry at being followed around by two much younger mediums who kept glaring at him, trying to figure out if he really had the gift or not.

I could see sweat beads building on my uncle's forehead and almost expected for him to faint. But he just pulled his handkerchief out and dabbed away, pretending that it was hot, even though we all could practically see our breath from how *paranormally* cold it was in the library.

If his cover was blown, I didn't know what would happen to our agency, so I pulled my camera out of my bag, turned it on, and tried to steal the twins' attention from Monty.

"Cool huh?" I practically shoved the display screen in their faces. Jessica looked down and tilted her head in interest. Jacob smirked and crossed his arms.

"You're pretty good at Photoshop, dude." I wanted to punch him in the face.

"It's *totally* not Photoshop, *duuude*," I was pretty good at being sarcastic when I wanted to be and this kid deserved it. Finally, he turned away from me and stalked off, yanking his sister along with him. She gave a faint smile before he whisked her off to the other end of the second floor.

"Good luck!" she waved before he could pull her behind a statue of Sherlock Holmes.

"They cost us a pretty penny," Jade swooped in beside me. She looked like something was bothering her and then I remembered just how insane these past couple of days had gotten. It seemed to be eating her up inside and I couldn't help but feel terrible. "Remember what I said about the camera," she added. "This time I'd recommend turning it off."

"Fine," I groaned, turned it off and shoved it back into my bag.

"Are you scared now?" Jade whispered as Monty plopped himself down in a chair and picked up a children's book.

I turned to her and pulled her to the side by the stairwell.

"I'm a little scared, to be honest." I tried to summon a smile. "I'm afraid of what's going to happen tonight. More afraid than I've ever been."

"Hey, there's something over here!" Jessica's voice rang out from the other side of the second floor. We all turned and hurried across. Before I could make it over to the twins, a gust of cool wind spun up my legs. It seized me by the shoulders and forced my head to look down at the ground. Written in dust on the hardwood floor was the same cursive writing from the window:

Follow the dust, come alone...

I looked up but no one else was paying attention to me. So instead of following them, I turned back to the dust and followed it as the words spun into the air and the dust particles led the way through the archway and into the back of the library's second floor.

I followed the dust, not knowing what I was doing.

What if this was a bad spirit? But then I remembered Jade saying that the writing on the window was the mute spirit she had told me about, the Lady in White. The dust stopped at a lone bookshelf that blended in with the back wall and then shot right through it, rattling a few books that were sitting on the shelf.

I'd seen too many movies to know what the next move would be.

"A secret passageway," I said aloud as the familiar gust of wind spun its way back up toward my shoulders and pushed me forward toward the shelf. A large green book wiggled by itself and without thinking twice, I took hold of it, pulled it back, and waited.

It took several moments but slowly the shelf began to rumble. I turned to see if anyone else was noticing but I was alone. The rumbling came to an abrupt stop, chunks of drywall were on the floor and dust clouded the air around me. I looked up and saw a gap behind the shelf, just large enough for me to slip through.

I waited, thinking about what would be waiting for me behind that shelf. Was it an entrance to my untimely demise? Or was there someone in there that really wanted to help? As if answering me, the gust of wind pushed me forward and before I could think about running, I had slipped through the gap and the shelf crunched shut behind me.

My eyes were closed and my heartbeat was pummeling against my ribs like a rabid monkey in a cage. I counted to ten before I let one eye slip open, my mind not prepared for whatever I was about to endure. After not seeing anything alarming in front of me, I opened the other eye and took in the scene before me.

I was speechless for a second and my heart was still going crazy in my chest, from both fear and amazement. I was standing on what looked to be a level of a secret library. Before me thousands and thousands of books sat collecting dust on what seemed like millions of bookshelves. I ran to the edge of the railing and looked over in utter amazement. It went on forever. There were hundreds of rolling ladders connected to shelves and each level had a railing and a tiny metal staircase that led up and down to each level. Murky sunlight poured like sapphire honey through three very large diamond shaped windows, giving enough light to see from my vantage point. Below, you'd either have to use a lantern or candle to see anything.

Realizing that if by chance these old railings didn't

hold correctly, I'd plummet hundreds of feet to my death, I pulled myself away from the railing and bumped right into something. An icy breeze wafted through my hair and I stood still, my heart picking up where it left off, beating against my ribs.

"No need to be afraid, young man." a strong male voice echoed slightly in the secret library. I didn't recognize the voice and I wasn't sure what I was going to turn around and see, but I had to remember one major thing that a priestess taught me in New Orleans: *Fearlessness is your greatest weapon against the paranormal.* So I sucked up my fear and spun around to meet whoever had brought me here.

Photo taken two months after grand opening.

CHAPTER 15:
REVELATIONS

I'd prepared myself to see something horrifying when I turned around. But instead I was met with the kind face of a much older man, in a much older suit. He smiled, his thin black mustache twitched as if it had a mind of its own. His hair was slicked back and I could smell something like car wax and almost gagged. If I had to estimate his death year, I'd say Victorian era for sure, which meant... I was in the presence of the man who was responsible for this house of horrors, *Jonathon R. Childermass.*

I cleared my throat and before I could open my mouth he spoke again, in such a clear and nonchalant tone that didn't carry any kind of darkness.

"I had one of my daughter's, Morgana, bring you here. I hope you don't mind about our meeting alone. Trust me when I say it is extremely necessary, young man." I moved out of the way as he walked over to a shelf beside me and pulled a large brown book from it.

He studied my face a bit more, probably trying to decipher whether or not he could really trust me. I was feeling the same way about him.

I couldn't stop staring at him. Normally full body apparitions aren't as clear and solid looking. You can see through them most of the time. Since it was rare, I almost wanted to reach out and touch him, but I didn't want to seem rude. He could walk the streets and no one would notice a thing.

"Are you..." I didn't get to finish, because he opened the book and pointed down at the same photo I'd seen while researching the library on the internet.

"Jonathon R. Childermass? I am." He smiled as he flipped to a few more pages and pointed again to a photo of three young women sitting on a couch, their eyes closed and their hands placed on their laps. One of them, the youngest, was wearing a veil that obscured her face. Another photo had two of the sisters beside each other, one didn't seem to have a mouth. One thing was certain. They were all dead. I swallowed hard. It was a Victorian custom to take photos of the deceased and keep them in death albums. Some people believed it was a way of keeping the soul trapped in the photograph so that it wouldn't be tormented on the other side, while some just thought of it as saving a memory of their loved ones.

"Who are they?" I asked, but then a cool chill rattled up my back and I knew there was someone else with us. I stood, paralyzed, as an arm reached over my shoulder and pressed a finger on one of the girls' faces.

I turned, nearly knocking the album out of Jonathon's hand.

A girl looking around the same age as Macy Parker was hovering a couple of feet away from me. Startled by my sudden turn she wavered a few more steps back, afraid of me. She was one of the girls in the album. She was dressed in a long white gown and I realized why Jade had told me she was mute. She didn't have a mouth.

"This is Morgana or as the locals like to call her, The Lady in White. She cannot speak as you can see, she was born that way." Jonathon sounded sad and I could feel his emotions like the sun on the back of my neck on a hot day. I was too open. I needed to find my inner anchor, which was the memory of my parents. I needed to hold on tight to that before I collapsed from all the energy they were sucking out of me.

I watched as Morgana pulled what looked like a tattered notebook out of a pocket in her dress and scratched at it with a tiny nub of a pencil. When she was done she held up the notebook and tapped at it with a finger.

You are in danger. My sister will stop at nothing to get what she wants tonight. Get out now, or you're just as dead as we are.

"*Sister?*" I asked and then it hit me. I spun back around to Jonathon, took the album from him, and flipped back to the photo of the three dead girls. I studied it closely and tried to figure out who the other older sister was and then it dawned on me.

I almost dropped the album in shock. Sitting next to Morgana... was *Octavia Freestone*.

"I... can't... I've got to go," this time I dropped the album on the ground and was about to make a break for it when Jonathon snatched me by the arm and turned me back to him. Where he held me, it began to burn as if someone was holding dry ice against my skin.

"She brought the spiritualists, including you, here to

sacrifice you to the Déjà Quimorta for more power. I tried to stop my own daughter before I died, but she found out and look at me now..." he was crying and he was draining me. I felt like I was going to throw up, but I pushed myself to stay alert. I couldn't faint now.

"This is too insane!" I yelled back at him.

"Your spiritual energy is what the demon Madolok craves and it will swallow you whole. You can't stop them... you have to get out of here while you can." *Madolok?* Why did that name sound familiar? I could feel the bile rising in my throat but I pushed it back down. Almost as if a spark had gone off in my head, a memory rushed to life:

I was in the hospital after the demon attack at The Diamond house. Monty was sleeping in a chair across the room, but someone was sitting next to me. It was a giant man with a long white beard and the kindest eyes... Emerson Lewis.

"Madolok... the demon's name is Madolok and it will never leave you alone until you destroy it with your own hands, Simon Santiago."

As if on cue, Monty awoke in his chair and the old man vanished before my eyes...

123

I looked up at Jonathon's face. What in the freaking heck was going on? And why was I such an important piece in this stupid puzzle?

"I don't know if I can do this," I said as I wavered and caught myself on the wall behind me. Jonathon pulled on me tighter, the pain from his ghostly grasp bringing me back to consciousness.

"Listen to me! Take your uncle and those poor innocent souls and leave this place. Do you understand?" I watched as a rush of pain seized Jonathon and he cringed away from me and began chipping away like the girl in the mirror. What was happening to the ghosts?

I turned to Morgana as she scribbled one last thing down. She held up the notebook and shook it in my face.

Get out!

I didn't hesitate for a second as I turned back to the shelf and pushed the wall open with all my might. I slipped back through into the library, breathless and more horrified than I'd ever been. I had to get everyone out before the eclipse began. I took another step, trying to push myself toward the voices of Jade, Monty, and the twins but my legs were like jello.

I hadn't made it a few more feet when a black cloud of fog appeared in front of me. I stopped in my tracks, and held onto the back of a reading chair. I was too weak for another encounter. I watched as a woman dressed entirely in black stepped out from the dark cloud and headed directly toward me. It was Black Veil. I'd finally come face to face with the big bad of the Childermass Public Library.

Poor boy, the spirit said in my head as it hovered closer. *You're going to die tonight and you'll finally be with your good for nothing parents.*

It was then that I realized that Black Veil wasn't a ghost after all. She was a demon... the same one that almost killed me in Texas. It told Octavia to bring me here. It wasn't done with me.

"I know something you don't know..." I teased it, still holding onto the chair. I didn't want to tell it the truth. I was too weak to fight.

YOU KNOW NOTHING! Black Veil's shrill voice tore through my head, feeling like it was shredding my brain into pieces. The demon moved closer until I could feel its tingly freezing chill penetrating my bones.

"I won't let you hurt anyone," I told it.

Two hours from now, you and everybody else will be dead and there is nothing you can do to stop me... I think it's time for a nap, don't you? The demon's voice echoed in my head as I tried to run. Suddenly as if recharged with energy I bolted back to the bookshelf and yanked on the green book. This time it wasn't budging.

The demon began to laugh behind me.

"*Goodnight, Simon Santiago.*" The voice wasn't in my head anymore and I could hear Monty calling out for me, wondering where I was. As if knowing she was about to be interrupted, the demon flicked her wrist and I watched as the light of the afternoon faded to pitch black.

Octavia & Morgana
Childermass

CHAPTER 16:
DEAD AFTER DARK

Someone was calling my name. It was soft and far away at first and then suddenly it was urgent and full of panic. It was a woman's voice and it seemed familiar. With my eyes still closed, I attempted to place it.

"Little Oso," The voice was closer now. My eyes filled with tears. It had been so long since I heard that name. Oso meant Bear in Spanish and it was the one nickname I let my parents call me.

"Mom..." I called out as I tore my eyes open. I was lying on a red couch in the children's section. I looked around me but didn't see anyone, I was alone. I blinked the tears out of my eyes so I could see better but I was still alone. The sun was still shining through the windows, tiny dusty particles fluttering in the warm beams.

I must've been dreaming.

"Simon... can you hear me?" it was my mom's voice

but it was distorted in a way. I jumped up from the couch and spun around, trying to find her, but no one was around.

"I can hear you!" I called out. "Why can't I see you?"

"Me and your papa aren't strong enough, mijo. But you need to be strong. It's not your time to be with us. There's so many more people you need to help..." her voice was wavering but I could hear every word and it made my chest hurt. I wanted to see my parents so bad. I wanted to be with them more than anything.

"I can't do this on my own," I said to the air, my eyes searching just for a speck of their existence. The warmth I was now feeling was familiar. The heart in the dusty coffee table made perfect sense now. They'd been with me the whole time.

"You're a Santiago, mijo. You're so much stronger than you think. Your papa's ancestry is so strong and powerful, you haven't even tapped into it all yet. You're unstoppable and people will come for you... like Madolok has... mijo, she's the reason we're not with you anymore. She took us from you."

My heart dropped into my stomach and I grabbed onto the couch to steady myself. I'd always thought it was an accident that took my parents away from me. But all along, it was a wicked demon with an appetite for Santiagos. I wanted to scream and break things. This was not right and it was not fair.

"I miss you guys so much," I cried into my hands.

"We miss you too..." this time it was my dad's voice. "But we don't want you to lose the same way we did, Simon." Whispering took over, a thousand different voices flooding the air around me. "It's time for us to go, Simon. If you don't make it out those doors before sundown, use all the strength you have in you and knock that demon's lights out, Little Oso."

"Wait!" I called out and jumped up from the couch. But they were gone... and this time, I wasn't alone. I was surrounded Jade, Monty, the twins, Rick, and Macy. The only person I didn't see was Octavia.

"You fainted," Jade looked worried for me. "We walked into the room where we heard someone talking and then you just dropped to the floor."

"You feeling okay?" Monty asked and even in the stress and confusion that surrounded me, I was surprised at his worry.

I needed to think. Why did my parents think I could take out a demon? I mean, I knew how to do it the basic way, though I wasn't a pro. But they finally came to me and if they believed in me enough to contact me from the other side, I had to believe in myself too. Without answering Jade or Monty, I walked over to the railing overlooking the first floor and gripped the metal tight.

"We need to get out of here before it gets dark," I said.

"Simon, you've been knocked out for the past couple of hours, the eclipse is already happening," Macy walked over to me. She placed a hand on my shoulder. But it didn't calm me down.

"Octavia brought me, you and the rest of them here," I gestured to the other Ghost Talkers. "She brought us here to sacrifice us to a freaking demon, Macy. Didn't you wonder why you were brought here right on time for the blood moon?" I turned to her and saw her expression morph from calmness to outright horror. She looked up at the windows and pointed at the tiny amount of daylight that was still pouring through.

"There's still a bit of daylight, which means we can

still get out of here," she turned to everyone else and clapped her hands. "Let's go!"

Everyone followed us as we hurried down the steps from the second floor. My heart was beating like crazy in my chest and I was sweating up a storm from how scared I was, but I needed to be strong. Just like my parents said I was.

"Simon, what the heck is wrong with you?" Monty grabbed me by the shoulder as I stepped down onto the first floor. I turned to him and prepared myself for him to get the angriest he'd ever be at me.

"If we don't get out of here now, we're all going to die. That demon, the one from The Diamond House, it's been after me since I was born. It killed my parents and now it wants me. It's here right now, Monty." I stared into his face, waiting for the rage to spark, but he looked just as scared as me. He understood, for the first time since I'd been with him, he understood. I wanted to hug him, but I figured it would be better if we were both still alive for that.

"Then let's get out of here." Monty ran up to the doors and yanked on the handles. They wouldn't budge. "They won't open!"

Destroy it with your own hands, Emerson had told

me that day in the hospital. Why had he told me to do destroy the demon with my *hands?* Why was he so specific? And then it dawned on me.

I hurried up to the doors and moved Monty aside. Wishing more than anything that I was right, I gripped one of the doors' handles and almost instantly it began to softly glow neon green. Smiling from ear to ear, I yanked on the handle and the door swung open and blue daylight spilt inside. It was my energy and it was more powerful than I ever thought it would be. That's why the demon wanted me. She wanted my energy and even if it killed me, she was never going to get it.

"Let's go!" I yelled out as the library began to rumble like an earthquake had just broken out. The demon knew we were trying to leave and it was getting angry. We needed to hurry.

I helped Monty wheel Rick out through the doorway as a strong gust of wind tried to blow him back into the library. Macy pushed the back of Rick's chair with all her might and made it out over the threshold and down the library's crackling steps. The demonic wind was too strong, but we had to get everyone out. Next were the twins and before we could call them, they ran into the doorway and tumbled out onto the steps of the library.

I turned and saw Jade still standing behind us, twisting her fingers.

"I'm sorry I didn't tell you everything," I told her and she looked up at me and nodded. I could tell I had hurt her and it hurt me to know it. She wiped tears from her eyes as she walked toward the doorway, the wind ripping at her clothes.

"Wait," Jade stopped. "Where's Ms. Freestone?"

I looked at Jade and shook my head.

"She's the reason why all of this is happening, Jade." But she wasn't budging. Ms. Freestone had meant everything to her after her mom died and now she had to believe that the woman was evil incarnate from someone she barely knew.

"But... but she's my *friend*," Jade cried and stepped away from the door. "I'm sorry, Simon. But I have to get her." She was about to turn away when I grabbed her and pushed her toward the door again.

"PLEASE!" I yelled. She turned to me and saw the pain on my face and looked down at the ground.

She caved in and nodded. I reached out to grab her and push her through the door, but the wind beat me to it and threw her backward into the library. She skid across the floor and slammed into a shelf, knocking hundreds of books to the ground.

"JADE!" I cried. I tried to run to her but Monty stopped me.

"Simon, we have to go!"

"I have to save Jade. Monty, you have to go!" I yelled at him. For the first time ever I was watching him cry. Tears ran down his cheeks and his jaw was rattling.

"NO! I can't lose anyone else," he screamed and grabbed me by my shoulders. He was trying to push me through the doorway, but even if the wind had somehow let me through, I was holding my ground. With all my strength, I spun away from his grasp and pushed him through the doorway.

He landed on the steps next to the twins. I watched as Monty scrambled back up from the ground and ran at the doorway. The wind knocked him back onto the steps.

"I'm sorry," I told Monty. He stood up from the ground and stared me right in the eyes, something he'd never done before. It was then that I could see the true sadness that rested inside of him. He'd lost his family when he was just a kid and lost his brother when he needed him the most. I'd never been able to get into Monty's head like that and now it was like it was overflowing with everything I'd always wanted to know.

"No... I'm sorry, Simon. I've been a rotten person and a horrible uncle and I'm so, so sorry." When I looked into his eyes, I could see a bit of my dad in him and a warmness washed over me. *Be strong.*

"I forgive you, Uncle Montoya..." And before I could say another word, the door slammed shut right in his face.

I tried to open it again, but this time it wasn't working for me. I had to get Jade and find a way out of here. I turned around and hurried to where Jade had crashed into a shelf, but she was gone.

CHAPTER 17:
ALL IS REVEALED

"Jade!" I called out in a panic. I quickly looked around but she was nowhere to be seen. The daylight that had been coming through the windows had disappeared and was replaced by utter darkness. The only light that helped me see was the electric florescent beams that hung from the ceiling that somehow stayed on after the library's tremor. The blood moon had commenced.

"Stupid boy," a familiar voice rang out echoing in the air. I spun around to see Black Veil hovering above the ground. "You're mine now!"

"Where's Jade?" I yelled at the demon.

"She's no longer your concern!" she growled and the floor shook. "You've failed, Simon Santiago and I *won*."

"Correction," I said. "You *think* you've won." I was not about to let this stupid demon think it was better than me. I knew my strength now and I wasn't afraid to use it.

"You've got a lot of nerve speaking to me with such malice. I'm going to enjoy sucking all of the energy out of your puny body."

The demon walked over to where the chairs had been formed into a circle and snapped her fingers. Tall red and black candles huffed to life, each with a bright orange flame that danced in the chilling breeze Black Veil had brought along with her.

When all the candles had been lit, the reflection of the mural projected itself into the middle of the circle and began to glow. All of the chairs were now occupied by spirits, four I recognized as Morgana Childermass, Jonathon Childermass, the girl in the window, and the boy with the train.

The candlelight grew brighter and it was then that I noticed two dark masses on the ground inside the circle. I took several steps closer and dread washed over me.

On the ground lay the gagged and tied up bodies of Emerson Lewis and Madame Helena. The last several candles lit and I noticed another familiar face appear in the chair next to Morgana... *Octavia.*

Confusion clouded my thoughts as Black Veil started to laugh behind me. This didn't make sense. All this time it was Octavia. All the clues pointed directly to her. But if Octavia was sitting in the chairs with the other ghosts, then who...

Reluctantly, I turned back around.

Black Veil's head was thrown back in cackling laughter and chills ran down my spine. I'd been played with the whole time.

Tears stung my eyes as the demon stopped laughing and then stared right at me. I didn't want any of this to be real. I didn't want what I was thinking to be true. It just couldn't be. But as if the final piece of a puzzle had been set, everything suddenly became clear.

Anger, frustration, and betrayal, rose in me like a boiling pot. I grit my teeth, clenched my fists, and set my glare on the demon.

"Demon, show your true form!" I shouted. The familiar wind from earlier came back to life and began tossing books off of the shelves and popping light bulbs. I'd made Black Veil angry, just as I wanted.

"YOU WILL NOT TELL ME WHAT TO DO!" the demon's voice got deeper and ragged. A bell began to toll inside the library, echoing and rattling the windows. Why was there a bell inside of a library?

"What the heck is that?" I said aloud.

"Its ring signifies that it's time for you to die!" The demon began laughing once again. "Poor Simon Santiago! You couldn't save your parents... and now you can't save yourself."

The bell stopped and a reddish glow shined down from above me. I looked up and saw the runes lighting up one by one. I needed to stop Black Veil now or I was as good as dead.

But this demon was strong, too strong. Even if I knew its name, would I be able to banish it? It had taken almost everything away from me and I couldn't let it win, not now, not *ever*.

As if answering my questions, my dad's voice reappeared in my head: *Knock that demon's lights out!* And funny enough, that's exactly what I was going to do.

"MADOLOK!" I screamed at the top of my lungs. The wind got stronger and this time furniture was flying and shelves were smashing to the ground. The library was getting destroyed.

The demon stopped laughing.

"NO!" Black Veil screamed. Its voice was a mixture of a monster and a child. "PLEASE DON'T!" it began slamming its hands onto its head.

"MADOLOK, SHOW YOUR TRUE FORM!" I shouted at the quivering entity. Just like the ghosts it had been tormenting, pieces of it began to flake away until there was only a person in a tattered black dress and a moth eaten veil lying on the ground.

I watched as it stood up, wobbling from side to side. It lifted the veil, revealing its true form: a thirteen-year-old girl.

I understood now, all the clues pointing to her and the spirits, Madame Helena, and my parents trying their best to tell me what was really happening. Morgana and Jonathon weren't trying to tell me it was Octavia. They were trying to tell me that it was the younger sister in the photo. The one with her face covered by a veil... a *Black*

Veil. God, I can be such a moron sometimes.

"Jade...*Childermass*," I said, gritting my teeth.

She was crying now as if I'd taken a toy from her. I waited for her to stop acting helpless. She was just in her true form now, but she was still pretty powerful.

"I THOUGHT WE WERE FRIENDS!" she screamed at me. Her eyes were different now, almost catlike. She looked primal. I almost expected for her to prance on top of me and rip my face off.

"Friends don't kill their friend's parents!" I shouted back at her. She'd tricked me with everything, even letting me in on her emotions. It was all fake. She'd been using the power from the mural all along. I still couldn't believe that all along it had been Jade. I still didn't want it to be, but there she was, hovering above the ground, a sinister grin growing on her demented face.

No matter what I'd thought of her before, I could not let it stop me from putting an end to her reign of terror.

"Why did you do all of this to me?" I asked. The wind was dying down because she had less power, but the runes were still being lit one by one and there were only several left. I was wasting time trying to understand why she did what she did. She was a demon, she didn't have a soul.

"Because... it was *fun*." She shook with laughter once again, her eyes glowing like spirit orbs in the dark. She's not a real person, I had to tell myself. She must've attracted a demon's attention when she was alive and when she died, she let it have her soul and take over her form. Whoever Jade Childermass was, she'd left a long time ago. I'd heard about stuff like that before, but never had I seen it firsthand. This was absolute insanity on so many levels.

"You're going back to hell, Jade! Or should I say Madolok!" I told her and she laughed even more, her high pitched voice slicing into my ears like razor blades.

"You're not strong enough, Simon. You may know my name but you will never ever be able to condemn me... you're just a sad little boy with dead parents and a deadbeat uncle who cares more about counting the money in his wallet than ever loving you!" she was trying to hurt me, but it wasn't working and as I stepped into the sacrificial circle, her demeanor switched from vicious glee to straight up concern.

"Remember when Madame Helena asked you to go

get that purple bag out of that room?" I asked Jade as I picked up piece of broken light bulb and wiggled it between my fingers.

"So what!" she grinned, trying to play off that she wasn't worried about what I might be doing.

"See, she casted a spell over that room and when you came back it was like you'd been gone a minute or two... but it was longer and during that time gap, she told me how to *really* destroy the *Déjà Quimorta...*" I could see the realization hit the demon and it was one of the best feelings in the world.

I smiled as I jammed the piece of glass into my right palm and then slammed my bloody hand onto the reflection of the runes. I began rubbing at them like a pencil eraser. I waited a moment, hoping that what Madame Helena had told me was true and surely enough, they began to crumble away and chunks of the actual mural above began to flutter to the ground like burnt pieces of paper.

"NO!! STOP!!" Jade shrieked in a monstrous voice that shook me to the core. But I didn't stop. More pieces of the mural fell to the ground, this time actual chunks of the ceiling were coming down, but didn't land anywhere inside the circle.

"Say bye-bye to your precious portal!" I yelled out before I rubbed my hand over the final rune and the building began to rumble once again. This time, the wooden floor began to crack and splinter.

"I'm going to kill you, Simon... just like I did your parents!" faster than I had anticipated Jade sprung into the air and headed straight toward me.

She slammed head first into what looked like an invisible force field.

"I can only hold it for a minute longer..." I turned and saw Octavia holding her palm out toward the ceiling, a light green beam of light hovering above her. "She's controlled me, these spirits, and my family for too long, Simon... Send her back to where she *belongs*."

"YOU DARE TO BETRAY ME, SISTER?" Jade bellowed at Octavia.

"You're not my sister! You don't belong in this world. None of us do." Octavia was losing her strength. I needed to end it all now.

I gathered up all of my courage, anger, sadness, and

soul and stood up from the ground. My energy was bubbling at the surface. With a vicious glare set on Jade's feral eyes, I held my bloodied palm out at her and readied myself for all the energy I was about to use.

"MADOLOK..."

"NOOOOO!" Jade threw an entire bookshelf my way but the force field knocked it back with a bang. I couldn't stop. I had to keep going.

"MADOLOK... IN THE NAME OF THE FATHER, THE SON, AND THE HOLY SPIRIT... I BANISH YOU BACK TO HELL!"

All around us, windows exploded inward, glass and metal flying all over the place. The walls groaned as if they were going to combust and the shelves crumbled to chunks of wood. I turned and watched as the second floor crashed to the ground. I could see the secret library perfectly now.

The spirits held captive were now vanishing into orbs and flying out through the shattered windows, finally released by the demonic presence that had been keeping them here for so long.

I turned back to Jade and stared her straight in the

face as she began to disintegrate just like this building. She gave me one last look of mercy before she crumbled away into black dust, her scream still lingering in the air.

It was over. It was all *over.*

I wobbled over to a chair and fell into it, exhaustion pulling at my mind and body. Something fell from above and landed softly on my chest. Using what little strength I had left, I grabbed whatever it was and looked down at it. It was Morgana's notebook and written in her beautiful cursive handwriting were two, simple, but *strong* words:

Thank you

EPILOGUE:
CASE CLOSED?

I was standing in front of the library once again. But this time, there was nothing dark or sinister lurking inside of it. It was basically all rubble now and the only thing left standing was the front of the building. The windows were blown out but the doors were somehow still intact.

I couldn't help but feel worse about the books that had been destroyed than the demon that masqueraded as a friend of mine and had been trying to kill me all along. I helped all of the spirits that were stuck in the library get free and that filled me with so much happiness. I made my parents proud and I proved to myself that I could do anything if I put my mind... *and* soul into it.

"Are you ready? You've been standing there forever!" Monty called from his idling Buick. I smiled back at him.

It had been a few weeks since I'd knocked the demon's lights out and Monty and I were finally getting on good terms with each other. Things were getting better, I noticed that right away.

After I'd woken in the hospital for the second time in my life, Monty had been right there waiting for me to wake up. He was trying, and that was really all I could ask for. But I knew with time, we'd be just fine.

"There's just one more thing I need to do," I said as I pulled my camera out of my bag, which somehow survived the library's paranormal demolition. I held it up to take one final picture of the library.

I focused in on the building and snapped a good photo of the Childermass Public Library, or what was left of it. I smiled as I looked down at my display screen and didn't see a single spirit.

"Let me ask you something, kid," Monty turned down the radio in his car and I turned back to him. "How did Jade and Octavia get past your ghost radar?"

"Honestly, I still don't really know. I think I might need to pick at Emerson's brain to find out more about that. I'm thinking it might have had something to do with how much energy Jade was consuming from the portal. She was using the power to make herself and Octavia more human. I mean, she fooled Emerson and Madame Helena and that's pretty serious. But it's a load of craziness that I'll just have to figure out eventually."

"That's some pretty heavy stuff, isn't it?"

"Yeah... it is."

As we drove through town for the last time, we passed Madame Helena's cottage and Ghost Town Souvenirs. I was going to miss Madame Helena and Emerson. But they told me I could always come back and visit, which I promised to do.

A tiny spark of electricity stunned the middle of my chest as we passed the *Now Leaving Childermass* town sign. I peered down at my camera, still dangling around my neck and pulled it off of me. Maybe it had suffered at the library after all.

The display screen was on and the photo of the library began to flicker and become distorted. I watched as the malfunctioning stopped and then I looked down at the photo once again and my eyes grew wide in shock.

Standing in one of the front broken windows was a white silhouette. Almost instantly my heart dropped into my stomach and I nearly dropped the camera on the floor of the car.

"Everything alright?" Monty said as he changed the radio station and nodded along with a new song.

I didn't know what to do. But as I looked back down at the photo, the silhouette was gone, which probably meant that it wasn't from the library... it was something else entirely and it was trying to tell me something. But right now, I didn't want to deal with a single ghostly thing. I just wanted to be happy for as long as I could. I'd dealt with the paranormal for so long that I felt I deserved a much needed break from all this chaos and that was exactly what I was going to do.

So I turned the camera off, took the battery out, and tossed the camera into the backseat. I looked over at Monty and smiled.

"Yeah... everything's just fine."

Turn the page
for some exclusive
B-roll photos from
Simon's camera!

Simon's Cam
B-roll Pic #1

Simon's Cam
B-roll Pic #2

Simon's Cam
B-roll Pic #3

Simon's Cam
B-roll Pic #4

Thank you:

I want to take this cool looking page I made to thank YOU, the person reading this book. Whether you bought it, borrowed it, or illegally downloaded it, I want you to know that it means everything to me that you would take the time to give my book your attention. Whether you end up hating it or loving it, thank you from the bottom of my heart.

— Richard

RICHARD DENNEY resides in Texas. He enjoys reading, writing, pizza, horror movies, making YouTube videos & fending off wicked demons with bad hairdos in his spare time.

Exclusive paperback
hint for book 2:

SCHOOL BUS